K.R. KEEN

The Weight of Glass

a Psychological Suspense Novel

First edition

ISBN: 979-8-9953164-0-4

This book was professionally typeset on Reedsy.
Find out more at reedsy.com

Chapter 1

She sat beneath the October sun as it hung lazily in the sky, its golden rays filtering through the auburn and amber leaves that clung to the branches above. A warm glow settled over the small patio where Heather and Benjamin were seated, each with a steaming cup of coffee nestled in their hands. The gentle breeze stirred, tousling Heather's vibrant red hair, causing it to dance around her face like flames flickering in the wind. Benjamin couldn't help but admire her as he tucked a loose strand behind her ear, his touch light.

It had started as a joke, meeting him at work instead of a proper date, but somewhere along the way, it had become theirs. Quieter than anywhere she'd expected.

Heather closed her eyes, soaking in the warmth of his touch. His calm demeanor soothed her agitated thoughts. Moments of peace beneath the shadow of the oak tree, but dark thoughts loomed dangerously close.

This patio always surprised her; so close to the hospital's sliding doors and the distant rhythm of machines, and yet somehow untouched by the rush. The faint scent of antiseptic drifted through the sweet aroma of roasted coffee beans, a reminder that the walls behind her still hummed with sickness and recovery. A cart rattled somewhere inside. The sound of a phone ringing carried faintly through the open doors, its tone steady and sterile.

A nurse crossed the courtyard with a clipboard; the pages fluttered and flashed like a pair of wings.

"You know," Heather said in between sips of coffee, "this place is surprisingly peaceful. I expected more chaos."

"You came at the right time," Benjamin's grin deepened, "Give it ten minutes, and it'll remind you where you are."

"And how does all that chaos make you feel, Dr. Benjamin?" she shot back, laughter dancing in her voice.

"Honestly? It makes me feel like a rock star performing for an audience of one."

Heather rolled her eyes, "Rock star, huh? I don't see a guitar or a crowd of fans."

He lifted his spoon and gave the rim of his cup a soft tap. "Improvising."

She squealed, shaking her head. "Please, no coffee solos. You'll scare the nurses."

Benjamin settled back down and took a sip of his coffee, a playful grin spreading across his face. "You know, I think that last sip was the best part. It's like a little celebration at the end of your drink."

Heather chuckled, her fingers tracing the rim of her cup. "So, are you saying the best part of me comes at the end?"

"Considering you haven't even finished it," he teased, "I guess I'll have to make do with your company instead."

"We're really doing this, aren't we?" she murmured, half-teasing, half unsure what "this" even meant yet.

Heather wrinkled her nose playfully, "I was waiting for the perfect moment. Coffee is an art, you know?"

"Ah, yes," he replied dramatically, "the fine art of letting it get cold while engaging in existential discussions about our lives."

She swatted his wrist and took a careful sip. A car alarm chirped and died on the far side of the lot. Somewhere, a door clanged shut; the sound bounced through the courtyard, then thinned against the brick.

Ben watched her lift her cup, taking a hesitant sip. "So… any plans for tonight?"

"I might just curl up with a book and pretend I'm somewhere else," she said, glancing towards the hospital entrance, where the automatic doors kept opening and closing, opening and closing, like a mechanical breath.

Benjamin studied her face, the way her mouth tightened just a little when she watched the doors. "Sounds perfect. But if this place has taught us anything, it's that reality is often messier than any book can depict."

Just as Heather was about to respond, Benjamin's phone buzzed against the iron table. The sound ricocheted off the stone and metal. He frowned as he glanced at the screen, the color draining from his face.

She met his gaze, concern knitting her brow. "What is it?"

"Sorry, a news alert," he said, voice even but clipped. "Something just came through."

Heather lifted her eyes. "Everything okay?"

He hesitated, scrolling. "Another body was found this morning outside Smithsdale. They're calling it the fifth Autumn Murder."

It carried weight, thick and metallic in the air.

"They think it connects to the older cases. They're reopening the investigation." He paused. "Your father's case is listed."

Heather's eyes widened, her hand tightened on the handle of

her cup until the heat bled through her skin. "Reopening?" she repeated, voice small. "After all this time?"

The patio opened up around her - no walls, just air and sunlight that didn't seem warm anymore.

"Yeah." Benjamin's tone softened, but he didn't look up from the phone. "They're asking for anyone who might've seen something back then to come forward."

The table, the cup, the light; they all slid away. Sound dulled, then sharpened. The smell of coffee thinned into something sour, familiar.

Static.

Her mind was already moving, the world tipping. A darkened room. The TV hissing snow. A bottle rolling against the wooden floor, its mouth chattering against a hollow place beneath the couch. The cheap liquor soaking through a thin, gray sock. Red where red shouldn't be.

The static grew louder until it filled her head, drowning everything else. The hospital's intercom hum blended into the hiss.

Her throat closed. Her hands went cold even as the coffee steamed against her palms.

"Heather!" Benjamin's voice broke through the haze, low and steady.

She blinked, the patio snapping back into shape. Her heart thudded too hard, too fast.

"It's happening again," she whispered. It came out smaller than she meant it to.

The edges of the courtyard wavered, branches shifting like shoulders in the corner of her eyes.

"Hey," he squeezed her hand, "Stay with me. Just breathe for a second."

She nodded slowly, though the knot in her stomach tightened. "One headline," she said faintly. "That's all it takes."

"No," he said gently, reaching across the table. "It's just hitting you all at once. It doesn't mean anything's happening right now."

"It's not weakness," he told her. "It's proof you remember too clearly."

A voice on the hospital intercom switched from background murmur to the flat clarity of protocol. "Attention staff, please remain in place while we conduct a brief security check."

The announcement's neutrality should have been reassuring, but it sent a ripple through the courtyard. Nurses gathered clipboards; a security guard appeared by the main gate, speaking quietly into a radio. Doors sealed with soft clicks.

Heather's breath caught. "Why does it always sound worse than it is?"

"It's standard," Benjamin said, but his eyes stayed on her face instead of the doors. "Routine maintenance or a drill. Happens more than you'd think."

Inside the building, a gurney squealed against linoleum, a monitor beeped, then stopped. Routine sounds, but each one struck her nerves like a signal.

She tried to laugh it off. "Great timing. Maybe they're trying to test my progress."

"You're doing fine. You didn't spiral. That counts."

After a few minutes, the intercom crackled again, dismissing the check. The courtyard returned to its usual rhythm, though Heather couldn't shake the tremor that had started under her skin. The sun had shifted behind a cluster of clouds, tinting the courtyard with a muted gold that made everything look slightly distorted through the glass doors.

She reached for her cup again. It had gone cold.

"I can come by tonight," he offered, tone light. "Just to check on you."

She hesitated, the thought of a quiet room suddenly less appealing than ever. "Fine," she spouted out too quickly, then after a beat, softly: "Just a little while."

The silence hung heavy between them, the sound of leaves whispering secrets in the background.

"I should head back," Heather finally broke the silence, her eyes drifting towards the courtyard path. The distant wail of a siren broke through the quietude, a reminder of her past.

Benjamin's brow furrowed. "You know it's probably nothing. Just… stay cautious."

"Yeah. Right," Heather replied, her voice barely above a whisper as she rose from the table. With one last glance at him, she turned and walked away, the unease settling inside her like a persistent fog.

* * *

The walk back to her building took less than two minutes, but the quiet always grew heavier once she stepped inside. Her place smelled faintly of jasmine from the pillow and something sharper underneath it. The muted light of the late afternoon filtered through her window, casting long shadows across the space. Heather sat cross-legged on her bed trying to read, but every small sound of footsteps outside or a door clicking shut somewhere nearby pulled her out of the story.

"Get a grip," she told herself, and set the book face down.

A quick knock echoed through the room before the door

swung wide. The creak sent her heart racing, but when she turned, Ben stood in the doorway. He leaned against the frame, one hand steadying himself, while the other cradled an old chess set.

"Ready for some serious strategizing?" he asked while shaking the box.

"Knock next time!" Heather exclaimed, forcing a laugh to shake off the tension. "I'm too young to have a heart attack."

"Where's the fun in that?" he retorted, stepping fully into the room and closing the door behind him. He placed the chess set on the bed between them, the glossy board gleaming under the fading light. "It's been a while since we had a proper match."

Though still jumpy, the sight of the chessboard sparked a flicker of excitement within her. "Alright, let's see what you've got," she replied, trying to mask her unease.

Time warped, each move pulling them deeper into the board's world. Heather was momentarily safe, nestled in the layers of strategy and tactics, lost amid the rhythm of captured pawns and strategic gambits.

"How are you feeling?" Ben hesitated.

She inhaled sharply, the memories clawing their way back. Memories of police sirens, the harsh scent of antiseptic, and the hollow echo of her father's absence.

"I can't help but feel… paranoid. I don't know. I just can't shake this feeling that it's not over."

Ben leaned back, leaving the game behind momentarily.

"Which is exactly why we need this little distraction." Ben nudged a knight forward. "Your move."

They fell into the rhythm—openings they both favored, exchanges they both knew to avoid. The board had its own logic, nothing to interpret, no shadows that could be mistaken for faces. Minutes lengthened. The sun dropped behind the neighboring buildings.

"Check," he said, too pleased with himself to hide it.

She nudged her knight over the check, buying a little time, then glanced toward the window. A dark shape crossed the sidewalk two stories down. Just a passerby. Just a hoodie. But her spine went rigid until the shape moved past the frame and did not return.

"Heather?" Ben's voice was gentle, like tapping a fish tank without scaring the fish. "Earth to my favorite opponent."

Sighing, Heather leaned back against her pillows, her heart rate finally slowing. "Sorry, nightmare brain."

"Understandable." He advanced a bishop and sat back. "You should call your sister."

Heather's fingers tightened on the knight. "Why?"

"She reached out. She's worried."

"Worried?" The word caught in her throat. "Where was that when—" She bit the sentence in half and swallowed the pieces. "We're not doing this."

Ben didn't move. "You're angry. That's fair."

"She left," Heather said, trying to keep her voice in the same room with her. "So I learned not to need her."

Silence pressed for a count of three. A pair of teenagers passed on the sidewalk, their laughter floating up, bright and ordinary.

"People crack under grief," Ben said finally. "Sometimes that looks like leaving. Sometimes it looks like staying and breaking anyway."

"Do you practice these lines?" She tried to laugh, and it almost worked. The board blurred, all edges and squares, then sharpened again. She slid her rook, steadying herself.

"Checkmate," he said a few turns later, softly this time.

Heather stared at the lost chessmen spread across the bed. "Worried," she said, testing it again. "Where was she when—" She stopped, jaw tight. "You have no idea what that felt like. Waking up in strange places, wondering if anyone would notice if I vanished."

He raised his hands, not in defense but in surrender. "I don't. You're right. But shutting everyone out won't change the past."

"I don't need a lecture." Heat built under her skin. "Not now. Not—" She looked down at her hands. They were steady. That felt like a small miracle.

In that moment, her resolve wavered. She sank back into her pillow, burying her face in her hands. "It's just so hard," she confessed. "Two days ago, I was fine, and now… another murder, another headline. It's like it never ended."

Ben watched her quietly, his fingers tracing the edge of the chessboard, then retreating as if he wanted to reach for her but thought better of it. The gesture was small, but she caught it anyway.

She got up, arms crossed, and walked toward the window. The glass caught the dim light; her reflection ghosted in it. She could feel Benjamin's eyes on her, full of empathy, yet all she could hear was the thrumming of her own heartbeat, beating louder with each passing moment.

"You don't have to decide right now," Ben said softly, moving closer until he was just behind her. "But think about it. Maybe reaching out could give you some closure or at least clarity. She is your sister."

Heather turned to face him, her heart pounding. *Closure* and *clarity* echoed in her mind like a haunting melody, making the flutter of unresolved emotions dance within her. She gazed up into Benjamin's deep brown eyes, searching for strength in the quiet depths.

"I'll think about it," she whispered, her voice barely above a breath.

He leaned down, resting his lips gently on her forehead – a tender gesture that sent butterflies fluttering in her stomach. It was harmless yet charged with something deeper, something unspoken between them.

Benjamin pulled away, wearing a softly lit smile that reached his eyes in a way that made her pulse quicken. "That's all I'm asking. Just think about it. You deserve to find peace."

He backed away toward the door and paused. "No matter what, I'll be here for you," he murmured before disappearing into the hallway.

When the door clicked shut, the seam of light along the floor faded to black. Heather turned toward the window, waiting to glimpse Benjamin at the sidewalk below. But instead, she caught sight of a man in a dark hoodie rounding the corner— his face lost in shadow. A blink later, he was gone.

It could have been anyone.

It could have been no one.

"Everything is fine," she whispered.

Chapter 2

Remembered moments tugged at Heather as she paced the bedroom, her fingers gliding across shelves that held the remnants of her childhood: a once-pink plush piglet, now the soft gray of age; a delicate snow globe with an ice skater twirling along an unyielding surface; and a well-worn photograph capturing a moment of joy that now seemed impossibly distant.

The room seemed to hold its breath around her. The radiator clicked at odd intervals, a metal throat clearing in the walls. The curtains breathed with a draft from the window that never opened more than a hand's width. Dust motes drifted lazily in the strip of lamplight, rising and falling like ash in slow water. The clock on the dresser ticked with a measure of patience that made her feel hurried, even standing still.

She lifted the piglet by its frayed ear, thumb rubbing along a seam she used to worry between her fingers whenever she was thinking hard. Even now, if Heather closed her eyes, she could hear the quick, bright loop of Holly's laugh down a hallway that no longer existed, the sound ricocheting from door frames, calling her to shared trouble or shared plans. She pressed the pig close to her chest and let herself imagine the weight of her sister's forehead against hers, the way they used to stand head-to-head and breathe the same breath before doing something brave or foolish.

She set the piglet down with care and picked up the snow globe. The skater inside was tilting eternally on one leg, the other lifted behind in a clean line, arms flung wide as if she believed the surface beneath her would one day soften. Heather tilted the glass and sent a mild blizzard tumbling around the small figure, glitter clinging to the tiny red scarf as it settled. No matter how often she shook it, the skater landed back on the same thin layer, polished and unforgiving.

A photograph leaned face down beside the globe. She hesitated, then turned it over. Her parents stood beneath maple trees in mid-turn, copper, rust, and gold crowding the air around them as they tossed leaves into the sky. The girls, two red-haired daughters in corduroy coats, reached up for the falling color, mouths open in laughter you could almost hear. Her mother's cheeks were apple-bright, her eyes crinkled at the corners in excitement; her father had one hand on each of their shoulders in that easy way that said this is mine, this is us, this is everything.

That happiness had been snatched away far too early, starting with her mother's illness and culminating in her father's murder, one of the several that autumn, the ones people in town still whispered about.

She pressed the edge of the photograph against her lip until it stung. *The day of their mother's funeral, it had rained and rained, the sky a mirror of their sorrow. The tent over the grave snapped and sighed with the wind. Holly had pulled her russet hair back in a tight band that made her eyes look larger and more wrecked. They had stood side by side, shoulder to shoulder, fingers overlapping, the way you hold on in a crowd so you won't be separated. "We'll be okay," she whispered fiercely, and Heather had nodded because her sister said it like a plan, like a map, like a promise.*

The days after were quieter than any Heather remembered. In the beginning, their father was simply a man buried in grief. He moved through rooms like he was made of steam. The television flickered soundlessly. Her mother's records stayed in their sleeves. The house spoke in small languages, settling boards, a tap left to drip, and his silence that grew like ivy over their lives.

Then the bottles appeared. Not many, not always. Just enough to blur the edges.

"Daddy's just sad," Holly would say, pulling Heather to the kitchen door so they could peer into the dim living room together. Their father's head would be tipped back, the lamplight skimming his throat. "He'll find his way," Holly would add, smoothing Heather's hair like she could smooth the world.

One night, the record player had come on all by itself, or at least that's how it felt. A familiar melody, one their mother loved, unspooled into the dark. Heather crept to the doorway.

"Daddy?"

He jolted, elbow striking the glass resting on the arm of the chair. It fell and shattered against the wood floor. The sound was a breaking star.

Her father looked at her, eyes wide like he'd been caught doing something terrible. Papers slid from his lap when he jolted, a thin stack scattering across the rug. He shoved them quickly back onto the chair beside him.

"Go to bed, bug," he said with a shredded voice.

She had stood there long enough to smell the sharpness of the liquor, long enough to memorize the way his hands covered his eyes as if he could erase himself in the dark behind his palms. Long enough for the sharp note of shattering glass to lodge somewhere behind her ribs and live there.

It didn't happen all at once. That's the thing people never understand when they talk about spiral. Grief is more creative than that. It finds new angles, new routes. It drips. It waits.

When a letter came from the college Holly had worked toward with the ferocity of a steady flame, they had celebrated with takeout and paper cups of flat soda, the kind of party you make with thin means and a full heart. "You're going," their father had said, jaw set with a stubborn pride that didn't fit with the slump of his shoulders. And she did. She packed up in a rain of notes and lists and taped-up boxes and kept telling Heather she'd call every day. "Every day," she'd repeat as if saying it would chisel a groove in time they could both follow. *"If you need anything, just run to the neighbor's house. Promise me."*

After that, the house took on a wider kind of quiet. On the night everything changed, the silence was engineered, as if it had been planned by someone with a cruel sense of humor. The air was too still. The wind pressed against the windows in slow, weighty pulses. She could hear her own breath as if it belonged to someone else.

A sound came from the den — a thud, then a scrape. She froze halfway down the hallway, hand on the door frame. *"Dad?"* she tried. It felt too small to do any good. Another sound, heavier. The lamp flickered. Her stomach turned to water, her limbs suddenly too light. A scream ripped the air.

Everything after that came in pieces, as if her mind couldn't bear to record the sequence. Lights at the windows like storms of color. Neighbors clustering, faces she knew turned into masks by the swing of red and blue. A woman's hands on

Heather's shoulders, guiding her backward so she wouldn't see. The smell of rain and mud, but also a hint of metal that sucked the spit right out of her mouth. She remembered the blur of the siren's pitch, how it changed as they arrived, and then settled into a steady pulse that made her skin feel too tight. In the back of the cruiser, her own reflection ghosted over the back of the plastic partition, watching her father become a public story; almost like a bad magic trick that didn't hide the workings at all.

Later, the station gave everything edges again; bright fluorescent lights that hummed like insects, a coffee smell with no warmth to it, angled chairs that were built for a different species. Men in uniforms spoke in lowered tones to Holly through a glass partition that made her look like she was underwater. The college sweatshirt Holly had pulled on over her pajama top was more like a costume than a lettered promise of a future that kept slipping out of their hands. When their eyes met, a terrible clarity settled there. Love, terror, guilt, a-too-adult kind of calculation. No words. Just that long look, and then Holly's gaze slid away as if she'd looked too long at an eclipse and couldn't stand the brightness anymore.

Days turned to months in a series of blank calendars. Heather kept moving because that was what muscles do when the mind can't. She learned to lower her eyes at the right times. To answer questions with as few words as possible. She ultimately learned that people liked a neat ending, even when there wasn't one.

Now, with the photograph in hand and the snow globe throwing faint moons on the wall, she tried to order the story so it contained fewer knife-edges. She put the photo back and listened to the building's small noises.

She drifted toward the window. Outside, the courtyard wore the night like it was made for it. The lamps turned the pathways into rivers of gold. The trees whispered their small secrets to one another, their leaves flashing every time a breeze lifted them. People were dots of motion passing by the empty benches. Tonight, the sky hung a little too low.

Should she call Holly? The idea lit up inside her like a match. Small and hot. It flickered dread and relief in equal measure. She thought about all the things she could say and all the ways it could go wrong. The bond they'd had was like a thread you could snap with a careless tug. But there was the other part too, the part that had held her after the funeral, the part that had rehearsed the call-every-day promise until it felt like a ritual. The part that could pick up where it left off if given half a chance.

She touched the piglet's ear again and felt a kind of permission in it.

The phone rang.

Gone was the sweet multi-note chime, the tiny rattle from the kitchen wall from her childhood. In its place came a single, practical ring, as if the phone had been taught better manners. It startled her anyway. Her heart did a graceless leap. She left her piglet and stepped into the hallway, already braced for something she couldn't name.

"Hello?" her voice hesitant and cautious.

A fragile crack, then a crisp, nasal voice found her. "Good evening, is this Heather Harper?"

"Yes, who's this?"

"Hi, this is Donna Bennett from The Smithsdale Sentinel. I hope I'm not catching you at a bad time." A pause that implied she knew she was. "We're doing a piece on the tenth anniversary of your father's case, The Autumn Murders, and I would like to interview you and your sister about it."

The hallway lengthened. The light overhead hummed louder. "I'm not interested," Heather said, heat rising up her neck. "That's not something I want to discuss, and you'd have to contact Holly directly to interview." She heard the scoff in her own voice and didn't care.

"Yes, I have been in contact with Holly." Donna's tone softened, rehearsed sympathy set to low. "She has agreed to meet with me."

Her thoughts stalled, then moved too fast. The idea of her sister sitting across from a stranger, talking about the worst night of their lives, was both impossible and exactly like something the world would ask of them.

"Does she not realize —" Heather started, a tremor splitting the sentence.

"I understand this is painful," Donna cut in smoothly. "Truly. Especially now that authorities have found another victim this morning outside Smithsdale." Paper rustled on Donna's end, a detail being placed just so. "They're reopening a number of the old cases and asking for witnesses to come forward. Your perspective could help the community, Heather. People remember the pattern. The autumn timing. The staging."

Heather's fingers dug into the phone's smooth casing until her knuckles ached. "Those murders have nothing to do with us."

"I hear you," with cadence of practiced care. "But the Department has broadened the window and is reevaluating overlaps. This could be crucial. Don't you want to help?"

What she wanted was air. Quiet. A version of the past that didn't keep rearranging itself under other people's hands.

"What I want is to be left alone." Each word measured. "You have no idea what this has done to me, or my family. You call me out of nowhere, stir this all up, and expect me to just go along with it? You've got no right."

"I'm sorry if –"

She did not want to hear the rest of that conditional apology. The receiver clacked against the cradle with a force that surprised her. The sound rang in the corridor, a sharp punctuation that made a door somewhere down the hall open briefly and shut again, curious and then not.

She stared at the phone, waiting for it to undo itself. The plastic trembled in its cradle, then stilled. Her breath came too fast. Her heartbeat had climbed up into her throat and was knocking there, demanding out.

She started to pace without meaning to. Back and forth. Four steps one way, a turn that brought her shoulder near the wall, four steps back. Each step made her feel almost buoyant, and the sensation upset her. She wanted weight. She wanted the gravity of certainty.

Donna's words looped in her head, a skipping record: another body, Holly agreed, ten years. It was like being dragged up the chain of a roller coaster.

Click.

Click.

Click.

Everything ratcheting tighter, the drop hidden just ahead but promised with each hard notch. She imagined Holly at some cafe table, fingers around a paper cup, a stranger leaning forward with a recorder and a sympathetic tilt to her head. She imagined a shadow at the window and the sound of her father's glass hitting wood, rewriting itself into something worse.

What would Holly say? She hadn't been there at the exact moment. She knew the shape of the night from phone calls and reports and the exhausted explanations of strangers. The unfairness of that rose like a tide and then receded, leaving behind the seaweed snarl of grief and love that never let go of each other.

She glanced at the clock. Late. Her thumb hovered over the number pad, and she imagined both outcomes at once: Holly picking up, Holly letting it ring. Holly saying her name with a sharp inhale, Holly saying nothing at all. She had to warn her. Even if it meant stepping back into that shared dark.

She exhaled and dialed.

One ring. The sound realigned her.

Two. Her pulse tried to keep time and failed.

Three. She thought of the snow globe; the skater suspended, one leg lifted as if believing she'd find softness.

Four. The line opened with a thin rustle, a breath, a shape of someone on the other end.

A stretch of silence so long she thought the call had broken. She could hear faint ambient noise; maybe a fan, maybe traffic, maybe just the blood in her own ears pretending to be the world.

A sigh threaded through. Then a voice she would have known in a crowd, even after all this time.

"Alright. Let's talk. When do you want to meet?"

The line hummed faintly against her ear.

Chapter 3

Fragments gathered themselves the way dust does in a shaft of morning light; sudden, floating everywhere once they've been seen. Heather paused with her fingers on the door frame, letting her breath even out before she stepped inside.

Dr. Powell's office was quieter than the hallway. The hum of the building dulled here, like sound refused to cross the threshold. The air carried a faint, clean scent she couldn't place, something mild that reminded her of distant rain. A single couch waited across from him, and a small table separated them. On it sat a notepad, a pencil, and a glass of water. Nothing else.

"Heather?" he said, standing as she entered. Late thirties, neat dark hair, sharp brown eyes softened by something practiced. "Good morning."

"Morning," she gestured.

"Wherever you're comfortable." He said, voice carrying that quiet steadiness people use when coaxing a bird to their hand.

She sat, her fingers finding the hem of her shirt. He eased back into his chair with the kind of stillness that moved like an interruption.

"How are you today?" he asked.

"In this moment?" she echoed softly. "I'm... here."

"Here," he repeated, like a point placed on a map. "That's a start."

The silence that followed wasn't uncomfortable; it was calibrated, like he knew how long to leave it before she'd fill it. When she didn't, he leaned slightly forward. "I thought we'd talk about what's been resurfacing. You mentioned feeling… fragmented?"

She nodded. "It's like fragments keep appearing, and I can't tell which ones belong where."

"Good." He said it gently, as if fragments weren't a confession but a compass. "Let's look at a few of them, one at a time. Start wherever you can."

Heather took a breath. "A reporter called me last night. Donna Bennett, from The Sentinel. She's writing about my father's case. The Autumn Murders." The words scraped her throat. "She said they're reopening old files because there was…another body found. She wants to talk."

He didn't write anything, though the pencil was right there. "And how did that feel?"

"Cold and exposed."

He nodded once. "Did she mention your sister?"

"She said Holly agreed to talk." The name felt fragile on her tongue. "That she already set something up."

"And that stirred what?"

"Anger." Heather's voice dropped. "And guilt. And maybe… jealousy." She exhaled. "I called her."

"Did she answer?"

"She did." She paused. "We're meeting today. In the courtyard."

His brows lifted slightly. "A good choice. Open air, familiar ground."

"I'm not sure I can face her." Heather's hand tightened on her sleeve. "She said she'd meet me, but I don't know what to say when I see her."

"Then don't start with words," he said easily. "Let the place hold some of it first."

She gave a weak laugh. "You make that sound easy."

He smiled faintly. "It rarely is."

He tapped the rim of his glass once before speaking again. The sound was soft but deliberate, punctuation rather than noise.

"You've mentioned someone who helps you find calm," his tone neutral but kind. "What is it about him that feels steady?"

She hesitated, sensing the edge of a tender thing. "When everything gets too loud, he…quiets it. He helps me remember where I am."

"That's good," Dr. Powell murmured, repeating her words the way someone might return a fragile object to its owner. "People like that can remind us what steady feels like."

The silence hummed like the pause between heartbeats.

"If it ever feels like too much," he added, "you can blame me."

She blinked. "Blame you?"

He shrugged, a trace of humor beneath the calm. "Tell anyone your therapist insists you take space. Therapists make good scapegoats."

She almost smiled. "You've done this before."

"Once or twice," the corners of his mouth lifting. "It works surprisingly well."

The stillness in the room softened around them. She almost forgot to be tense.

He leaned forward, set down his glass on the coffee table, "When you meet Holly, you don't owe her explanations. Just honesty. You can tell her you need time before talking about the past, or not tell her anything at all."

"I'll probably mess it up," Heather muttered.

"Then we learn something new," he replied, tone so even it might have been scripted. "If you need to step away during the meeting, use that as a boundary. Say I've asked you to. Step out, breathe, and come back when you can."

Heather nodded slowly. The idea of having permission to leave, of blaming someone else for leaving, was relief disguised as logic.

He studied her, then said quietly, "You're doing well," eyes holding hers for a beat too long. "More than you think."

She wasn't sure whether to believe him.

He reached for a small stack of blank paper and placed one page in front of her. "A simple exercise. Write the word *Fragments* at the top. Then, when memories come, write them in single lines. Don't chase the story, just list them as they appear. Each one gets a box beside it. When you've faced one and returned from it, check the box."

Heather touched the page but didn't take it. "Like labeling jars," she sighed. "Jars I don't want to open."

His eyes warmed. "Exactly. This gives them somewhere to go besides tangling together in your mind."

She took the page and folded it in half, careful not to crease it too harshly. "Okay."

"Good." He stood, signaling their time without saying it. When he opened the door, the faint hum of the hall returned.

Sessions like this always stretched longer on the way in than on the way out, she thought.

As she stepped through, he added softly, "And remember," the corner of his mouth lifting just slightly, "if you need to walk away, blame me."

Heather turned back, uncertain whether to thank him or question what that really meant. "Alright," she said. It came out thin, but it was honest.

Out in the corridor, the air smelled faintly of rain again. Heather kept the folded paper in her hand instead of reading it. The edges were already soft from where her thumb pressed too hard.

She hesitated at the corner, then folded it again, smaller this time, and shoved it into her pocket. A forgotten memento, maybe. Or something waiting to be remembered.

She drew a steady breath and started toward the courtyard.

Chapter 4

Of all the days for the sky to hold its breath, it chose this one.

Heather took one steadying breath and let it out through her pursed lips. She told herself she'd write when she was ready. She told herself she had control over at least that.

At the junction where the hall bent toward the courtyard, a narrow cart had been nudged against the wall, a handmade chalkboard sign clipped to its handle: TODAY: COFFEE / TEA. Beneath it, someone had written in a loopy hand, rain or shine.

A woman in a forest-green cardigan stood behind the cart, holding a stack of paper cups and a thermal carafe labeled "Chamomile" in blocky black marker. Heather hesitated, then drifted over, drawn by heat and the small ritual of holding something in her hands.

"Chamomile?" the woman offered, already reaching for the cups.

"Please." Heather watched the steam unfurl as the cup filled. The woman added a cheap wooden stirrer and a foil packet of honey with a tiny bee printed on it. Heather thanked her and slipped a dollar into the lidded jar; someone had drawn a smiley face on the lid, and the mouth dipped where the tape puckered.

She stood, paper cup pressed to the soft inside of her wrist. The warmth grounded her. On the far side of the corridor, a wall clock clicked forward. A door whispered closed somewhere behind her. If she pressed her palm to the glass, she could feel a faint vibration, as if the whole building were an animal breathing in its sleep.

She turned toward the courtyard.

The door pushed open with a rubber-sealed sigh. Damp air met her, no rain yet, but soon she noted. The square garden pooled with color that hadn't yet been washed flat: rosemary hedges, a low stone border around a bed of pansies, ivy crawling up the walls in dark green ribbed lines. A fountain at the center made a sound like a throat softly clearing, over and over.

She took the same spot she had last time, at the ivy-covered wall with a view of the gate. The paper cup trembled a little against her fingers until she braced her elbow on the table. She sipped. It was too hot and too sweet and exactly what she needed.

She caught it first in the reflection of the fountain's water. A figure at the gate, blurred and bending with each ripple. A moment later, the real shape followed, breaking free of the shimmer: Holly, hood drawn, came walking down the concrete path.

Even from across the stones, Heather could see the thinness of her and wanted to slide something warm around her shoulders. The same old ache rose in her, the one that swelled in places where childhood didn't fit anymore.

They didn't rush the last ten feet. They did not call names. It was the slow approach of people who had a lot to say and were terrified of saying any of it wrong. When they hugged, it was careful, their chins catching on each other's shoulders like they used to when they were little.

"Hey," Holly's breath was warm against Heather's ear. When she pulled back, her smile was tight, eyes bright with something that was not quite tears and not quite light. "You look…good."

"So do you."

They sat at the iron table. Holly tugged the damp edge of her sleeve, then shrugged off her raincoat and folded it over the back of the chair, a small act of control.

Neither of them spoke. The fountain's slow rhythm filled the silence. Holly's gaze wandered to the ivy, the way the leaves twitched in the wind like a nervous tick. "It smells like rain." Her voice stayed low, as if that were safer than anything else they could name.

Heather nodded. "Always does." She traced the paper seam of her cup with her thumb.

"She texted," Holly announced. "She's here already. I told her we needed ten minutes."

Heather nodded. "Thanks." She took another sip from the flimsy lid, felt the paper go soft against her thumb where a seam pressed.

"I thought," Holly started, then stopped. Her gaze flicked to the notebook bulge in her bag, then to Heather's face. "I thought we could set some boundaries. Before she sits down."

"Okay." Heather's voice sounded strange in her own mouth. "No photos. No last names. No…kids. We don't talk about your kids."

"Agreed." Holly's relief was physical; she exhaled, shoulders dropping a fraction. "And if it goes sideways?"

"We can stop," Heather declared. "We can leave."

It loosened something inside her chest, like a knot worked

with patient fingers.

Holly gave a quick nod, grateful. "There's something else," she added, eyes going softer, wary. "If she asks about anything personal, you don't have to answer."

Heather nodded, though *personal* landed like a pebble in her throat. She turned her cup between her hands. The tea had cooled enough to drink; she didn't.

"I thought about calling." Holly's voice cut back into the quiet, sudden and brittle. "After Dad. After... everything. But every time I picked up the phone, I didn't know what to say that wouldn't make it worse."

Heather's fingers tightened on the cup. "You could've said anything."

"I know." Holly's eyes dropped to her hands. "I was scared the wrong thing would come out."

Heather held her gaze. "And now?"

"Now I'm scared of saying nothing," Her laugh cracked before it reached her eyes.

That earned the smallest smile from Heather. "So, same problem. Just new stakes."

"Story of our lives," Holly murmured.

They shared a small, real laugh. It didn't close the distance between them, but it cracked a window in it.

Then a small shift in the light caught her eye. A shape paused at the gate, without grace or hesitation, moving with the short, efficient steps of someone used to being unwelcome and coming anyway.

Donna Bennett.

Heather had seen her picture bylines before; small square faces beside narrow columns, but in person, Donna looked more...condensed. Short, heavy-set, brassy hair scraped back into a no-nonsense twist. Lines bracketed her mouth, but not from laughing. Her expression had the permanent squint of a woman who'd been up too early for too many years. Her shoulder bag dragged at her frame, overstuffed and uncaring.

"Afternoon," Donna didn't bother to sound cheerful. Her voice had a dry, nasal edge, like paper being folded. "Holly. Heather." She nodded at each of them, eyes already cataloging. "Thanks for meeting me."

She didn't sit until she'd unzipped her bag, pulled out a thin folder, a battered notepad, and a small digital recorder. The motions were practiced and efficient. She set the recorder on the table, then the pad. The pen went on top, click-ready.

"I've got a consent form," she recited, sliding a sheet toward them and dropping a cheap ballpoint beside it. "Standard stuff. You can end the interview at any time. If you say 'off the record,' I stop. No photos. Audio and notes only. That work for you?"

Her tone made *consent* sound like a box on a checklist.

Holly drew the paper toward her. "No last names in the story," she consented. "No mention of the kids. No speculation about our dad beyond what's documented."

"Fine." Her pen hovered. "First name, last initial, then. And I won't name your children. That's not what this is about." She glanced at Heather, not quite meeting her eyes. "You can read the draft before it goes to print. I don't promise to change everything you don't like, but I won't blindside you."

It was, technically, a kindness, although it sounded like policy.

Heather signed, the pen making a faint scratching sound that reminded her of police forms, of stations and statements, and fluorescent hum. Holly signed next. Donna took the paper back without comment, folded it in half, and tucked it into the folder.

She clicked the recorder on. The red light glowed, small and accusatory.

"Okay." No preamble, no throat-clearing sympathy. "Let's start with the basics. Ten years ago, your father, Daniel Harper, was found dead in your home off Oakview. Official cause of death: blunt force trauma. Manner: homicide. The case, as you know, was never fully closed."

Heather's hand tightened around the cup. Her tea sloshed, a quiet wave.

Donna's gaze flicked from the pad to the recorder. "Heather, you were eleven at the time. You were the one who found him." She didn't soften the word. *Found.* "Can you walk me through that evening from your perspective? Just the sequence."

Like memory could be reduced to steps. One thing, then another, with nothing underneath.

Heather's tongue felt clumsy. "It was late." Her throat tightened. "I was in my room. I heard a sound. A...thump. Then scraping." She swallowed. "I thought Holly had come home."

Donna's pen moved, quick and efficient. "Time?"

"I don't know." Heather stared at a crack in the tabletop. "After midnight. Before one. I didn't check the clock."

Donna nodded once. "Okay. You heard a thump, then scraping. You thought your sister was home. Then what?"

"I went to the hallway," the courtyard swam, then steadied. "The TV was on...with snow. That buzzing sound. There was a bottle on the floor. It rolled when I stepped. It..." She broke off.

Holly's hand closed around hers under the table, firm, as if anchoring her to the metal grid.

"That's enough," Holly inserted.

"It's fine," Heather lied automatically.

Donna's expression didn't change. She made another line on the pad. "So the television was on when you entered the room," she repeated. "You heard…snow. Static."

"Yes."

"And the bottle was already on the floor?"

"Yes."

"Full? Empty?"

"I don't know." The questions were like fingers in her mouth, counting teeth.

Donna gave a small grunt that might have been assent. "Okay. Holly, you were at college, out of town. You received a call from the police. How long after the incident?"

Holly blinked, focusing. "I don't remember the exact time. It was the middle of the night. One-something. Maybe two."

"But not before one," Donna injected, pen ready.

"I don't know," Holly repeated, irritation flashing. "I wasn't looking at the clock, Donna. I was trying to understand why someone was telling me my father was dead."

"Right." It sounded like a box being ticked. "Emotionally distressing. Of course."

Emotionally distressing landed with all the warmth of a medical note.

She moved on. "So, for ten years, the case has remained in that status: unsolved, under review. Recently, as you're aware, another body was found just outside Smithsdale, matching certain aspects of the Autumn Murders pattern. The department has reopened several files, including your father's."

Holly flinched. Heather stayed very still.

Donna looked between them, more interested in the reaction

than the pain behind it. "The community has…questions," she continued. "About overlaps. About timing. About whether the Autumn Murders are really done, or whether they were ever properly understood in the first place."

"'Community'… meaning you." Heather's tone was flat.

"And others," Donna replied, not bothering to deny it. "I'm not here to accuse your father of anything. I'm here to ask what it has been like living in the shadow of that night while the official story keeps… shifting. Heather, has the department contacted you directly since the new body was discovered?"

"No," Heather responded. "Just you."

Donna made a small note. "So you're hearing developments from the media, not from investigators."

"Yes."

"Does that feel… frustrating? Disempowering?"

Heather stared at her. "It feels like being rehearsed for the same play every few years without ever getting to leave the stage," she retorted. "Does that answer your question?"

"Partially," Donna snorted. She didn't look up. Her pen scribbled something that wasn't that sentence. "You've both repeatedly denied any connection between your father's death and the other Autumn cases. Given the coroner's window on Hannah Kline and the rough alignment with your 911 call, are you still comfortable saying there is no possibility of — "

"We're not talking about theories," Holly cut in. Her voice was calm, but her jaw was set. "You said this wasn't about that."

"I said this wasn't about blaming your father." The distinction was so technical it might as well have been written in a policy manual. "Patterns matter. People want to know they're safe."

Heather's tea had gone cold. Her fingers had gone hot. "People want a story that lets them sleep," she scoffed. "That's not the same thing."

Donna finally met her eyes. Her own were tired, ringed with the yellow-gray of someone who lived on caffeine and fluorescent lights. "Stories are how people understand their fear," she retorted. "You know that, whether you want to or not."

Heather saw the human under the job. The woman who had listened to a hundred families like hers and gone home with other people's nightmares clinging to her clothes. Then Donna flipped a page, and the moment was gone.

"Two quick things," Donna's voice went brisk, businesslike. "One: there's a mention in an internal note about a piece of paper found in your father's jacket pocket. It is not in the public report. Do you know what it said?"

The courtyard constricted. Heather's grip crushed the paper cup, tea seeping through the seam.

"No." The truth was a knot. "I don't."

Donna's pen didn't pause. "No one told you? You never saw it? Holly?"

Holly shook her head, lips pressed together.

"Okay," Donna muttered, as though verifying an address. "Second thing: the room. I've seen partial descriptions. The TV on static. The bottle. The placement of the body. Some details are… reminiscent of the other scenes."

Heather blinked. "Scenes," she repeated. "Like in a movie."

"Crime scenes," Donna corrected, tone flat. "Technically."

She flipped a page, the sound sharp as tearing paper. "But what's interesting is the pattern. Every Autumn Murder victim was positioned a certain way, surrounded by personal objects. "In your case —" her eyes flicked to Heather, pen poised, "a bottle, a television, and a photograph turned facedown. It almost looked…arranged."

Arranged slid between them like a blade.

Holly's chair scraped an inch. "We're done." Her voice had gone tight. "You've got enough."

But Donna leaned forward, elbows on the table, voice low and falsely sympathetic. "Heather, sometimes people who discover the body — children, especially — rearrange things without realizing it. Shock does strange things to the mind. Do you remember moving anything that night?"

Heather's pulse roared in her ears. "What are you implying?"

Donna's smile didn't reach her eyes. "Nothing at all. I'm just trying to understand the truth."

"One last question." The faintest edge of impatience now. "Then we can wrap, and I'll leave you alone."

"You won't," Heather snapped, even though she knew what Donna meant was physically, not existentially.

Donna ignored that. "If the department asked you to testify, or to sit with a profiler to reconstruct that night, would you be willing? Yes or no."

The fountain kept clearing its throat. The cloud above them pressed lower. Something in Heather's chest snapped with an almost audible delicacy, like thin glass bending too far.

"No," she barked. "Absolutely not."

"Is that because you don't remember?" Donna pressed, clinical. "Or because you don't trust what they'd do with the truth?"

Holly's voice cut in, sharp. "Okay, that's enough. Turn it off."

Donna didn't move. The recorder's red eye stared up at them. The pen held still in her hand. Then she reached, clicked the button. The light went dark.

"There's clearly more here." Her tone was matter-of-fact, as if she were remarking on the weather. "If you change your mind —"

Heather stood so fast the chair legs shrieked against the cobblestones. Birds startled from the ivy; a few leaves let go of their grip and spun down.

"You want more," Heather protested. Her voice didn't sound like hers. It had gone thin and sharp, an edge honed by ten years of hearing other people tell her story back to her. "You want details, you can type between ads for hardware stores and fall festivals so people can cluck their tongues and say *what a tragedy, what a shame*, and then sleep better knowing it didn't happen to them."

Donna's mouth flattened. "People have the right to under-stand what happened in their community."

"They have the right to shut their doors and feel safe," Heather scoffed. "They don't get that from you dissecting the worst night of my life like it's a puzzle in the Sunday insert."

Donna's fingers tightened on the pen. "My job is to ask questions," she jabbed. "You agreed to answer some. You did. I appreciate that."

"You don't appreciate anything." Emotion finally burst, hot and humiliating. "You tolerate. You record. You reduce. That's all."

Holly rose too, reaching for her. "Heather —"

"I can't do this," Heather said, not looking away from Donna. "I can't sit here while she pokes at dad like he's a pattern and not a person. I can't."

She left the cup where it was, leaking slowly onto the iron lattice. The sky above pressed even lower as she crossed the courtyard, like she could reach up and smear the cloud with her palm.

She walked.

Not quite running. Not strolling. That narrow speed in between that says *if I stop, I'll shatter.*

The covered walkway took her in. The shaded concrete was cooler, the air thicker. Her breath sounded too loud in her own ears.

"Heather!"

His voice arrived before he did. It was cutting through the static in her head with the familiarity of a song she knew all the words to. She kept moving, pretending she hadn't heard, but her shoulders had already reacted, drawing up and then dropping in recognition.

Ben.

"Heather, hey." Footsteps behind her, then beside her. He didn't grab her arm. He matched her pace like he'd practiced it in the past. "I saw you leave the courtyard."

Of course, he had. Of course, he always saw too much.

"I'm fine," she whispered, which was practically a reflex. It came out raw.

"Mm," He hummed, noncommittal. "You're walking like the floor's made of knives. Want to try something else?"

They reached a wide support pillar, and she stopped there, one palm flat against the cool paint. Her forehead followed, resting lightly. The world swayed around her as if it were on a gimbal.

"Ground with me?" he asked, voice low. "Five things you can see."

The phrase rang with an odd familiarity, like a line from a dream she'd had more than once.

She forced her eyes to focus. "The sky," she muttered. "What little there is." A gray rectangle framed by the edge of the awning. "The ivy. The chipped paint at the bottom of this post. Your…" Her gaze dropped. "…your left shoelace."

He glanced down. Sure enough, one loop had worked itself loose again. A quick huff of surprise escaped him, almost a laugh. He knelt automatically to tie it.

"See?" he said, looking up as he finished. "Evidence I'm not infallible. That's four. One more."

She scanned the ground, breath trembling. "The little plastic cup," she said finally, nodding toward where one had been crushed underfoot near the walkway, half-flattened and glinting with a film of rain.

Ben followed her gaze, the faint smile softening his face. "Good. Something small and real," he said gently.

"Three breaths?"

They did them together. First one shallow, barely in. Second, a little deeper, her lungs protesting like she'd asked them to move furniture. Third one full, down to the place where panic sits when it's not screaming.

"Two things you can feel."

"Sweat. My heart where it shouldn't be."

"Okay," he murmured. "One thing you can hear."

She listened. The fountain, muffled by distance. Somewhere, a cart wheel squeaked.

"You," she said finally. It was the only answer she trusted.

His throat moved as he swallowed. He opened his hand, palm up, not touching her, an invitation rather than a demand. "Want to get off the walkway?" he asked. "I'll order food."

She nodded and didn't let him see the way her throat clenched on the nod.

They didn't talk much on the way back to his office. Sometimes that was the kindness. The halls had a way of carrying voices forward to people who were not ready to receive them. A maintenance cart whirred past with an orange light blinking. The driver didn't look up. A poster on a bulletin board fluttered in the humidity — the corner had lost its tack and folded over, hiding Tuesday until it flapped back and revealed it again.

In his office, the air was both familiar and strange. Dimmer than the hall, softer. The faint green of eucalyptus still clung to the space; the same scent that always seemed to find her lately, no matter where she went. Basil and takeout containers would compete with it soon enough.

On the low table beside the couch, a single glass of water sat sweating on a coaster, half-full, as if someone had set it down mid-thought and forgotten it.

Ben nudged the blinds so the slats lined up perfectly, a small ritual she'd watched a hundred times. "I'll get plates." He dropped his keys on the desk with a soft clink. "You can sit. Or pace. Or dismantle my book order. Dealer's choice."

He stepped out. The room exhaled with him gone.

Heather sat on the couch anyway. Her body had learned the shape of this seat, the way the cushion dipped slightly more on one side. That was when she noticed the picture frame.

It sat near the corner of his desk, angled toward where she sat.

Two figures caught mid-movement, the blurred edge of motion softening their outlines. The image was slightly washed in light, the details harder to hold onto the longer she looked.

They were dancing.

Someone must've taken it quickly, without warning. The overhead lighting in the photo cast a warm halo across their faces.

But she knew that shoulder.

That tilt of the head.

The way he held someone when he was listening, not leading.

Her breath caught.

He'd never mentioned having the picture of them, like that.

But then again, he didn't have to.

Some moments lived on their own.

Ben returned with plates, oblivious to her gaze on the photo.

"Thai okay?" he asked, even though he'd already placed the order. "They know me now. I'm pretty sure I'm single-handedly funding their expansion plans."

"Fine." It was more than fine.

The food arrived in a rustle of paper and the soft knock of a delivery at the door. Ben paid with a quick, muffled thanks. He spread the cartons across the table between them. The air warmed with steam and spice — basil, chili, something star-anise sweet.

They ate in silence at first. The kind that wasn't empty; just tired.

"I can't believe how she kept pushing the Autumn Murders…" Heather said eventually, starting at the tangled noodles she'd wound around her fork. "Like Dad was a… a data point she can slide into whatever pattern suits the story this week."

"Local papers love a pattern," Ben finished a bite of curry. "Doesn't mean there is one."

"She kept saying 'community' like she meant 'crowd,'" Heather muttered. "People deserve to feel safe. People have questions. People want context." She stabbed at her noodles. "People want to watch other people bleed and call it staying informed."

"People also want something to blame for the feeling they're already unsafe," he mentioned. "It's easier if it's a mystery killer with a spooky name than... statistics and systems and random chance."

"It's easier if it's my father," Heather scoffed, the bitterness catching her by surprise. "Dead men don't sue for defamation."

Ben didn't flinch at the acid in her voice. He nudged the carton with the spring rolls towards her. "That's an excellent point," he said. "And an excellent excuse to eat your feelings via deep-fried vegetables."

She huffed. It wasn't quite a laugh, but it leaned in that direction.

He picked up a pair of chopsticks, then paused. "Full disclosure," he eyed the chopsticks. "I have no idea what I'm doing with these."

"You ordered Thai." Her brows lifted... "You didn't think that far ahead?"

"I thought as far as noodles," he admitted solemnly. "Then my brain clocked out." He attempted a bite. The noodles slid away, landing unceremoniously back in the carton. "See? Tragedy."

A small, reluctant laugh escaped her. It loosened something hot and tight in her chest.

"Better." His voice stayed quiet, more observation than praise.

She traded him her fork for his chopsticks. "Here," she giggled. "I'm the noodle engineer now. You can tackle the spring rolls. With your hands. Like an animal."

He gasped. "How dare you?" He took one anyway, biting into it with a sigh that was only half exaggerated. "I'm a professional, I'll have you know. I just happen to be deeply unprofessional around food."

"Clearly," she smiled. But the sharpness had gone from her tone.

"Okay," a laugh punched out of him. "Real talk. When I first started here, I spilled red curry down the front of a file folder that had to go to records by five. I dried it under the hand dryer in the men's room and then had to explain to Facilities why the bathroom smelled like lemongrass for a week."

Heather pictured it: Ben in a tie, hand under the dryer, praying nobody walked in as he held a manila folder like sacrament. She laughed again and shoved the extra food containers toward him. "You're a menace."

"A menace with integrity."

She took a breath. The room steadied. The burn behind her eyes faded to a low ember she could cup her hands around without scorching her palms.

The silence had changed. Gone was the brittle edge from before; this quiet settled over them like a blanket.

It made sense that her legs ended up stretched across his lap without her remembering how they got there. It made sense that his hand drew idle shapes on her calf, not greedy, not apologizing, just tracing the fact of her.

They had never named what this was, and maybe that was part of why it worked.

"Is this wrong?" The question was bigger than the room, like she was asking about more than this.

He didn't pretend he didn't know what *this* was.

He took a breath, watched it leave him.

"I'm thinking about lines," he admitted, "About timing. About not hurting you. About not confusing safe with easy."

She nodded. "I don't feel confused."

Then, because honesty had been a thing between them since the second day, she added, "Much."

"I want to take you somewhere with ridiculous little umbrellas in the drinks," he chuckled. "I want to watch you order too many and then insist you're fine."

"I would be fine," she exclaimed with dignity that made him grin outright.

"I like... this." His hand squeezed lightly, once. "I also like you not getting hurt by this. Those are not always the same thing."

Her chest ached. "I don't feel hurt," she whined. "I feel... found. For once."

He smiled a little, "You're very good at saying the most dangerous things like they're completely reasonable.

"Is that a compliment?" she urged.

"Ask me again in ten years."

The phone on his desk buzzed. They both jumped. The sound cracked the moment like a knuckle.

He glanced at the screen, mouth tightening. "They've been calling nonstop today," he muttered, half to himself. "Probably about the conference schedule next week. Everyone's scrambling to finalize travel." He exhaled, then looked at her again. "This one's a patient, though. I need to check."

"Of course," she sighed, even as something inside her sagged. "Go. Save the world."

"I was aiming for 'competent paperwork,' but sure, let's call it that." He stood and squeezed her knee. "I'll come back, if that's okay."

She wanted to tell him that every time he left, the air forgot how to breathe.

Instead, she nodded. "Don't take too long." She hated the way it sounded needy.

His eyes softened. He leaned in, his breath warm near her temple. "I'll try." Then he checked his shoe, noticing that his left lace had worked itself loose again. "Seriously?" he muttered, crouching to tie it. The sight made her want to laugh and cry at once.

The door clicked shut behind him, a soft, considerate sound.

Silence settled back over the room, rearranging itself into something almost gentle. The cartons on the table sagged as the food cooled. The glass of water still sat on the coaster, half-full, a faint crescent where someone's lip had touched it earlier.

Heather shifted, reaching for the pen on the end table beside the lamp. Her fingers brushed the grain of the wood. The eucalyptus note in the air wrapped around her. It could have been comforting or clinical. She didn't want to decide which.

She pulled the folded page from her pocket and unfolded it on her knee.

Her hand shook once. Then steadied.

She began to write:

-Rain against the tent at the funeral.
   -Dad's glass shattering on wood.
   -Blue and red lights through the window.
   -Do you know what it said?
   -The photograph faced down.
   -Voice in two rooms, same words, different man.

The last line startled her. She hadn't meant to write it. It sat there anyway, black and unblinking.

She stared at it until the ink looked shiny, then dull. Her chest climbed and fell. Nothing exploded. The ceiling stayed where it was.

The relief came quietly; a subtle loosening, like one notch let out on a too-tight belt.

She folded the paper again, careful not to crease it too deeply, and slipped it back into her pocket. The pen went beside the lamp. She gathered the empty cartons into the paper bag, rolling the top down, tucking their mess out of sight.

When she stepped into the hallway, the building had shifted toward evening. The light had gone warmer, shadows pooling in doorways. Somewhere, someone laughed. A cart rattled. A nurse walked past with a stack of folders, eyes on her list.

No one looked at Heather. For once, she was grateful to be just another shape moving through the corridor.

At the stairwell, she paused and listened to the pipes talk in their wet, secret language. The storm outside was still thinking about it. So was she.

She took the stairs down. Each step made a small, solid sound. At the landing, she glanced up through the square window. A single drop slid down the glass, drawing a hesitant line. Another followed, slower, as if they were both still deciding.

She smiled, barely. No one saw it.

In her room, she hung her jacket on the back of the chair and set the folded page on her desk.

Her shoes came off with small pops. She lined them up side by side, toes facing the door. The overhead light was too bright, so she switched it off and let the muted gray from outside take over. The room softened, corners rounding.

She stood at the bathroom doorway, hand on the frame, feeling the cool of the tile seep through her socks. The idea of the shower rose in her mind with almost painful clarity — steam, water pounding so loud it drowned out everything else, the clean blankness of fog over glass.

"Okay," she told the empty room.

She turned the handle. The pipes shuddered, then sang. Steam climbed the mirror.

She stepped in.

Chapter 5

Truth was supposed to cleanse, not sting.

Hot water pounded the back of Heather's neck, steady as a fist. She let it, standing hunched under the stream until her skin prickled a little too much and the spray blurred into white noise. Steam thickened the air, curled past her shoulder, climbed the bathroom mirror until her reflection vanished behind a soft, shifting veil.

If she stood here long enough, maybe today would dissolve.

The courtyard.

The recorder's red eye.

"Arranged."

Holly's hand gripping hers under the table.

Do you remember moving anything that night?

She pressed her palms flat to the tile, fingers spread. The grout lines were faint beneath them, a small, fixed pattern against the relentless rush of water. A trickle snuck down her forearms, along the inside of her elbows, slipped into the hollow at the crook, and disappeared.

Her breathing tried to match the water's rhythm and failed. Each inhale was thin. Each exhale caught on something sharp inside her chest.

Fragments surfaced, out of sequence.

A bottle rolling, the sound of glass against wood.

Blue and red lights flashing on neighbors' windows.

Holly's voice on the phone last night.

Donna today, leaning forward with that tired, hungry look. Some *details are...reminiscent of the other scenes.*

Heather squeezed her eyes shut. The water hit her lids, rebounded in hot little needles at the corners. Her scalp throbbed where the spray struck the same spot over and over, but she didn't move. Pain felt easier, in its own way.

"Stop," she whispered, but it drowned immediately, swallowed by the shower's roar.

She tried to wash the day off in layers.

First, Donna's voice. She imagined it sliding down her shoulders, under the spray, spiraling toward the drain where the sudsy water was already gathering, clouded with soap and heat and the faint lavender scent from her body wash. Then Holly's face, the tight smile, the way her eyes kept flicking to the recorder as if expecting it to bite. Then the word *note.*

A piece of paper found in your father's jacket.... Do you know what it said?

Her stomach flipped. That one didn't wash away so easily. It sat between her ribs like a wet stone.

The water fogged her ears a little, muting the sound of the building to a soft, underwater thrum. She almost let herself sink into it, into the illusion that nothing existed beyond white tile and steam and the small, enclosed world she could see.

Then a sound slipped through.

Not the metallic thunk of pipes. Not the thin tick of the bathroom fan. Something else.

A dull noise, padded around the edges.

Heather's head snapped up. Water hit her face, rushed over

her lips, and into her nose. She coughed, turned half sideways, listening. Every droplet was louder now, hiding anything else that might be there.

"Old building," she muttered, but the reassurance slid right off. "Neighbors. Upstairs."

As if in answer, another sound. Soft. Heavier than a drip, lighter than a slam. The kind of noise that might be a body leaning back, or a bag eased onto something.

Heather reached for the faucet without looking, fingers fumbling along the slick chrome until they found the handle. She twisted. The stream cut off with a squeal, leaving a hidden vacuum of quiet that made the room tilt.

The silence on the other side of the bathroom door was different now. Less like rest, more like someone holding their breath.

It could have been nothing.

It could have been him.

Water still dripped from her hair, down her spine, off her elbows. Each drop that hit the shower floor sounded too loud. She could hear her own breathing in short, jerky pulls.

She grabbed the towel from the hook with fingers that weren't quite steady. The terrycloth was rough against her palms, heavy as she wrapped it around herself, tucking the edge tight across her chest. It clung where she was still soaked, cool air sneaking into the damp spaces.

She just stood there, toes curled against the bathmat, ear angled toward the door.

Nothing. Maybe. Or everything.

Except nothing, didn't usually come twice.

The memory rose without invitation: a hallway that smelled like spilled liquor and rain, the distant hiss of a television on the wrong channel, her hand small on the door frame. Her father's voice, slurred and falling apart. Then no voice at all.

"Not now," she breathed. "Not here."

She reached for the knob. The metal was cool, a little slick under her damp fingers. She turned it slowly, easing the door open just wide enough to peer through the gap.

Her room was dim, washed in the bluish light of an evening sky pressed low against the window. Shadows stretched long from the dresser to the far wall. The chair with her jacket draped over the back sat exactly where she'd left it. Her shoes were lined up neatly by the door, toes pointing out like obedient children.

The bed wasn't empty.

On top of the made quilt, along the side closest to the door, a large shape lay diagonally. One shoe lay on its side near the edge, laces a collapsed bow. The other foot, still wearing the matching shoe, rested on the blanket, ankle turned outward. An arm lay flung over the sleeper's stomach, the other hung slightly off the bed, fingers loosely curled.

Everything went still at the edges; the shapes didn't resolve into anything but outline and possibility. Her chest went tight. The room narrowed; the distance from door to bed stretched and shrank at the same time.

It's not him, she told herself. It can't be. That's not —

The figure breathed.

A slow, audible inhale lifted the chest under the wrinkled shirt. The exhale came with a faint, unconscious sound, halfway between a sigh and a snore.

Relief hit so fast her knees went weak. It didn't erase the fear; it flooded over it, left her a little dizzy, like standing up too quickly after lying down too long.

"Ben," she exhaled, the name catching on its way out.

His hair was the next thing she recognized. A dark, mussed mess flattened on one side and puffed up on the other, like he'd lost a battle with her pillow. His shirt was partly untucked, one sleeve rolled, the other still buttoned at the wrist. The knot of his tie was gone entirely; the top two buttons of his collar were open, revealing a triangle of skin at his throat. He lay on his back, stretched diagonally, as if he'd only meant to sit and gravity had done the rest.

Heather stepped into the doorway, letting it swing the rest of the way open. Her heart was still racing, but the fear had shifted from sharp to echo. She adjusted her grip on the towel with one hand, knuckling water off her eyebrow with the other.

He didn't stir right away. Up close, she could see the faint bluish half-moons of fatigue under his eyes, the roughness of stubble on his jaw. His lips were parted just enough for each breath to slip through.

Of course he came.

She hovered on the threshold, as if one wrong move might spook him back down the hall, might undo the fact that he was here, stupidly stubbornly here, in her room, on her bed.

"Ben," she tried again, a little louder.

His eyelids fluttered, once, twice. The eyebrow closest to her twitched as if trying to wake itself. He inhaled more sharply, rib cage lifting, then blinked himself slowly up through layers of sleep until his gaze found her.

He squinted, brows pulling in. For just a beat, she saw confusion there, the half-dreaming sort.

Then he focused. His eyes widened a fraction.

"Oh," he rasped, the sound catching in his throat. His gaze flicked down, then jerked back up to somewhere safely above her head. Color rose along his cheekbones. "Heather. Sorry. I —"

Her mouth tugged, the ghosts of fear and relief fighting for expression. "You're on my bed," she said. "In your shoes."

He looked down at himself like he needed proof. One hand patted the blanket, then found the offending shoe still on his foot.

"Half my shoes," he corrected, voice rough with sleep. "That's something."

He reached down and clumsily tugged the remaining one off, the heel slipping against the quilt. The motion nearly unbalanced him; he caught himself with his free hand, bracing against the mattress.

"I knocked," he added, glancing toward the open door and back. "A lot more times than is legally polite. No answer. The door wasn't locked." His eyes softened. "After today, that freaked me out a little."

She swallowed around a lump in her throat. "You could have waited outside."

"Could have," he agreed. His hand smoothed an imaginary wrinkle from the quilt. "Probably should have. Didn't."

Any other day, with anyone else, she might have bristled at that. Right now, after the way her heart had plunged at the sight of that dark shape on the bed, anger just… didn't rise.

"You look exhausted," she said instead. It came out somewhere between accusation and concern.

He gave a crooked half—smile. "I'm reassured my aesthetic matches my inner life."

The corner of her mouth lifted despite itself. The towel tickled the back of her knees; water droplets were sliding down her calves, making tiny dark marks on the floor.

"Can you…" she gestured vaguely toward her torso. "Not look for a second?"

His hand flew up immediately, palm inward. "Right. Yes. Consider me visually impaired." He squeezed his eyes shut for emphasis. "Fully clothed and mostly harmless."

"Mostly," she echoed, something lighter threading through her voice now.

She crossed the room to her dresser, the soft slap of her damp feet against the wood being the only sound between them. Even with his eyes closed, she could feel his awareness follow her, the same way she always sensed him entering a room before she saw him.

Drawer, cotton, the familiar weight of soft joggers and a worn T-shirt. She clutched them against the towel and headed back into the bathroom. The door clicked softly shut behind her.

Inside, steam still clung to the mirror. She leaned against the door, the cool wood at her back, and watched the vague shape of herself behind the fog. Damp hair clung in ropes along her shoulders; the towel's edge cut a pale diagonal across her chest.

The adrenaline began to ebb, leaving a strange hollowness behind.

"You're okay," she told the blurred reflection. "He's here. You're okay."

She dressed quickly, the T-shirt dragging briefly over still-damp skin, then settling. The joggers were soft on her hips, familiar. She twisted her hair up into a messy knot at the base of her skull, fingers working without much thought.

When she opened the door again, the room felt a fraction smaller, more contained. The world outside had shrunk to the rectangle of her bed and the space between it and the bathroom.

Ben still sat propped against the headboard. Both his shoes were now placed neatly beside hers on the floor. He'd straightened his shirt, more or less, though one side was still tucked, and the collar sat slightly askew. His head rested back, eyes open, staring at her ceiling as if it had something interesting to say.

He turned his gaze toward her, checking, not a steady sweep. He moved his focus carefully to her face and kept it there, as if everything he needed to know could be found in her eyes.

"Better?" he asked quietly.

"Drier," she replied, tugging at her hem. "Marginally more clothed."

He shifted over a little, making space. The quilt beneath him was still undisturbed, the corners square. He hadn't pulled the blanket back or burrowed under. He'd collapsed on top of her perfectly made bed and gone out like someone whose body had simply vetoed whatever his brain had planned.

It softened something in her she hadn't realized was clenched.

Heather sat on the edge of the mattress near his legs. The quilt dipped under her weight; his knee rolled a little closer to her hip. The proximity was new and familiar all at once.

"You didn't answer my question," he said after a moment. "Are you okay?"

Heather stared at her bare toes. A droplet of water slipped from the ends of her hair onto her ankle, cool against the warmer skin. She tracked it with her eyes until it disappeared into the cuff of her joggers.

"No," she said honestly. "Not really."

"Yeah," he replied. "Me neither."

Her head turned at that. "You?"

He shrugged, a small, tired roll of one shoulder against the headboard. "Turns out watching someone you care about get picked apart in public is not high on my list of fun recreational activities." His hand flexed briefly on his thigh. "I keep replaying all the parts I didn't interrupt."

"You couldn't have," she said. "Or…shouldn't have. It wasn't your place."

"That doesn't mean I liked it," he murmured.

The word *care* lodged somewhere in her, warm and sharp.

She let her weight tip sideways until her shoulder brushed his leg. The contact was light, a test. He didn't shift away. The warmth of him soaked through the cotton of her sleeve.

"Thank you for coming back.'"

He huffed softly. "You make it sound like some heroic trek. I walked down a hallway and fell asleep on top of your quilt like a raccoon in a laundry basket."

"That's a very specific image."

"Accurate, though."

She let her head tilt, resting the side of it lightly against his thigh. The position was more intimate than she meant it to be, but now that she was there, moving away was admitting to something she wasn't ready to admit.

His hand hesitated, then lowered. It landed carefully on her shoulder, fingers curling just enough to rest, not enough to hold.

"Long day," she murmured into the quilt.

"Longest in a while," he agreed.

They sat there in the half-dark, blues and grays pooling in the corners of the room.

Heather's eyes slipped closed. For the first time since the courtyard, her thoughts weren't racing somewhere ahead of her. They hovered, delayed, like they'd been forced to wait for a train that might never come.

"You remember," she said suddenly, without lifting her head, "what you said about those drinks? The stupid little umbrellas?"

She felt his eyes on her.

"From earlier?" His fingers brushed a damp strand of hair off her neck, almost absently. "Yeah."

"You said you might have to take me to a place that serves them," she went on. "If I kept eating Thai food like I was auditioning for a commercial."

"I recall something along those lines," he replied. "I also recall you threatening to drink as many as you wanted."

She made a small sound that might have been a laugh. It came out tired and real.

"We could still do that," she murmured. "You and me. Go somewhere that's not here. Some bar with bad lighting, an ocean poster on the wall, and cocktails with stupid names. Leave all of this behind for a bit."

He went quiet. His thumb traced a small, unconscious arc along the ridge of her shoulder blade through the cotton.

"We could," he said slowly. "Just…pick a direction and drive. There are probably at least three tragic tiki bars within a hundred miles. It's not exactly local, but close enough we can pretend."

She smiled into the quilt, "You say tragic like it's a plus."

"With you, it might be," he admitted.

She lifted her head, turning enough to see him properly. In the low light, his features were softened, edges blurred. His eyes looked darker, and his hair was messier than usual.

"Then let's go," she said. "Not forever. Just…for a while. Before everything else starts up." Her throat tightened. "Before they decide they want more from us. From me. From that night."

He watched her, and she could see it; the version of him who wanted to say yes without qualifiers — the one who would grab his keys, take her hand, and not look back.

Then she watched the other parts settle over the one like layers: responsibility, self-preservation, the simple fact of a life that existed beyond this room.

"I have to be gone for a couple of days," he said quietly. "Conference."

The word didn't belong here, like something dragged in from another language. Too bright, too bureaucratic.

"You mentioned calls," she said. "Earlier. When we were eating."

He nodded. "They finally pinned the schedule down this afternoon. Workshops. Presentations. All the things they think will turn us into better versions of ourselves if they cram us into a hotel ballroom and ply us with coffee." His mouth tipped. "I leave the day after tomorrow. Back before the weekend's over."

"So we can't run away yet," she summarized, staring at the pattern on the quilt. Small stitched diamonds, repeated, neat and predictable in a way nothing else in her life had been.

"Not yet," he said. "But after..." He shrugged, one corner of his mouth tugging. "Seems to me the umbrella drinks will still be there. Tragic tiki bars don't die easily."

She studied his face. "You're sure you're coming back?"

He didn't hesitate. "Yes."

"Don't say it if you're not."

"I'm not in the habit of lying to you," he replied. "Terrible long-term strategy, that."

She let that settle. It was ridiculous, as reassurances went. It still worked.

"Okay," she murmured.

He shifted, sliding down the headboard a few inches so his body angled more comfortably on the bed. His hand slid from her shoulder to the side of her neck, two fingers resting lightly in the hollow where her pulse thrummed.

"You're still breathing too fast," he said softly.

"Occupational hazard," she whispered.

"What occupation is that?"

"Survivor," she said, then wished she hadn't.

His thumb stroked her skin once, slowly. "You shouldn't have to work that hard at it."

Something in her chest cracked, like ice breaking on a river in spring.

She turned toward him more fully. Their faces were close enough now that she could feel his breath when he exhaled. It smelled faintly of toothpaste and the Thai basil from earlier, the combination somehow surprisingly gentle.

"Come here," he whispered.

She didn't ask what he meant.

When she shifted, the quilt wrinkled beneath her. She eased closer, the movement small but deliberate, her chest finding his as naturally as breathing. His arm adjusted automatically, making room, wrapping around her waist with a care that made her throat ache.

Up this close, she could see the tiny gold flecks in his irises, the faint line near his temple where his glasses sometimes pressed. His heartbeat thudded against her ribs, not as fast as hers, but not steady either.

They just looked at each other.

His hand slid up her back, fingers splaying between her shoulder blades, warm and reassuring. The other lifted to her face, his knuckles grazing her cheek before his palm cupped her jaw.

When he kissed her, it wasn't rushed. There was no crash, no frenzy. Just a slow, steady warmth that started at her mouth and spread outward, loosening knots she'd forgotten she tied. His lips moved against hers with a kind of hungry patience, the kind that made it clear he'd thought about this for longer than he'd ever admit.

She let herself fall into it.

The world shrank again, this time willingly. To the softness of his mouth, the faint rasp of stubble against her chin, the way his hand at her waist tightened when she sighed into him. To the tiny, involuntary sound he made when her fingers slid up into his hair, tugging lightly at the mussed strands.

Her pulse pounded in her ears, but it was a different kind of hurry now, one that turned her forward instead of sending her running.

She shifted closer, the line of her body fitting against his. His shirt was warm under her hands, the fabric thin enough that she could feel the heat of his skin through it. She slid her palms along his chest, up to his shoulders, feeling muscle and bone and the quiet strength there.

He responded in kind, his fingers tracing the hem of her shirt. When she arched into him, a silent yes, he let his hand slip under the cotton, fingertips exploring the curve of her spine with a reverence that sent a shiver down her back.

Heather's thoughts thinned to single words.

Warm.

Here.

Alive.

Somewhere, on the edge of her awareness, the day still existed. The courtyard. The questions. The note in the pocket. They hovered at the margins like static waiting to break in.

But every time they tried, something in the way he held her pushed them back. He didn't erase them. He didn't have that power. He just made it possible, for these moments, to set them down.

His mouth left hers briefly, traveling along her cheek, the corner of her jaw, the hollow just below her ear. Everywhere he went, he left a trail of heat that made her toes curl. Her hands roamed with more confidence now, tracing the familiar slope of his shoulders, the side of his neck, the place just above his heart where his pulse beat strong.

"You okay?" he murmured against her skin.

"Yes," she breathed. And she was surprised to find that, right now, it was true.

The bed shifted under their combined weight as they moved together, slowly, finding the rhythm that was theirs and no one else's. Clothes became more of a hindrance than a help. A shirt here, a sock there, her joggers pooling somewhere near the footboard. The quilt, stubbornly neat all day, finally surrendered and slumped to one side.

Heather didn't catalogue each piece. She noticed impressions: the brush of his bare arm against hers, the slide of her leg over his, the way his chest rose and fell more quickly when she traced a path down his side.

They didn't talk much. When they did, it was in pieces.

"Here?"

"Yeah."

"Too much?"

"No...don't stop."

Every so often, he paused just enough to search her face. Each time, she answered before he could ask, meeting his gaze, kissing him again, pulling him closer. Choosing, over and over, in every small movement, to be here in this room, in this bed, with this man, instead of anywhere else that history had dragged her.

When they finally went still, it was not the abrupt drop of a curtain, but a gradual settling. Heartbeats slowing. Breath stretching. The room expands again, including the corners, the ceiling, the soft whir of the fan pushing tired air around.

Heather lay on her back, staring up at the ceiling. Her skin hummed, warm and used, pleasantly sore in places that had forgotten what it felt like to be touched with that kind of care. Her hair long since come loose from its knot; it spread around her head in damp, dark waves.

Beside her, Ben lay on his side, propped on one elbow, head resting on his hand. His other palm sprawled over her stomach, fingers relaxed against the rise and fall of her breathing.

He looked softer like this, the angles of his face gentled by exhaustion and whatever had just passed between them. There was no smugness there, no self-satisfaction. Just a kind of quiet wonder and a bone-deep tiredness that matched her own.

She turned her head to look at him. "Hey," she whispered.

"Hey," he echoed.

They watched each other, saying nothing, the way people do when words would only drag something fragile into the wrong light.

He was the one who broke the silence.

"You know," he said, voice low, "if we ever actually get to one of those umbrella-drink places, I'm going to insist on the most ridiculous one on the menu."

Her lips curved. "Flaming volcano?"

"Minimum," he said. "Something with three kinds of rum and a warning label."

"You'd hate it," she pointed out.

"I'd love watching you hate it less," he countered.

She snorted, then winced as the small laugh jostled all her muscles. "You're ridiculous."

"Accurate," he agreed.

Her eyelids were growing heavy. The ceiling above them seemed farther away now, like someone had lifted it slightly in the night.

"Two days," she murmured, more to the ceiling than to him. "Then you're gone."

"Three nights." His thumb stroked an absent-minded path along her skin. "Not forever."

"I know." The old reflex, the urge to brace for abandonment, to pretend she didn't care, tugged at her. She let it tug and then let it go. "Call me if you can. When you're there. Or when you're bored. Or when the coffee's bad."

His mouth softened. "I will," he said.

"Promise?" It slipped out before she could catch it.

He heard what was really inside it. She could tell by the way his expression shifted, the way his eyes went a little more serious.

"I promise," he said. No dramatics. No oath. Just that.

It settled over her like a blanket. Thin, maybe. But it was something.

She let her eyes close briefly.

The drip in the bathroom had finally stopped. The building groaned once, somewhere in the bones of it, and fell quiet again.

Ben's hand on her stomach rose and fell with her breaths, a soft, steady weight.

Truth hadn't made anything easier today. It had cut her open in front of strangers and laid old wounds bare. It had pressed new questions into her hands she hadn't asked for.

But here, in the narrow space between his heartbeat and the fan's quiet hum, with the taste of his mouth still at the back of her throat and his promise lingering in the air, it didn't feel like an enemy.

Raw wasn't the same as ruined.

Heather drew in one last, slow breath, filling her lungs until the edges of her ribs ached, and let it out into the dim room.

For the first time in a long time, she let sleep come without bargaining.

Chapter 6

But the dream always starts the same.

The hallway stretches long and patient before her, the carpet thin from footsteps she doesn't remember taking. The air smells of damp wood and dust caught in fabric. Stale air that hasn't moved since that night. Her skin prickles, knowing exactly what comes next.

The light at the far end of the corridor blinks twice, steadying into a pale rectangle spilling from beneath the den door. The rest of the house sleeps. The hum of the refrigerator is gone. The clock has no tick. Only that light remains, pulsing faintly like a heart under gauze.

Heather stands barefoot, toes curling against the carpet's flattened threads. Her pajama hem brushes her ankles. Cotton, blue, thin with age. She's known this for years.

Her hands hang uselessly at her sides.

"Dad?" she calls softly, though the word isn't really a call anymore. It's just part of the ritual. She must say it for the dream to keep breathing.

No answer, of course. There never is.

The silence is thick. Too complete. She can hear her pulse inside it, slow and out of sync with everything else. The television hums beyond the door, a low static sigh she can feel in her ribs.

Heather starts forward. Each step leaves a shadowed print in the carpet. The floor creaks where it shouldn't. She tells herself she could turn back, that she's done this enough times, and that maybe the dream would let her leave now.

But the thought doesn't even make it to her hands. They lift on their own.

Her fingertips graze the wall as she passes, tracing the bumps in the paint. The light under the door flickers once. Her stomach tightens, waiting for the familiar shape that comes next. The outline of the glass on the table, the couch, the stillness.

The smell sharpens before she even touches the knob: whiskey, sweat, the faint metallic undertone that makes her teeth ache. It fills her throat, sweet and sour and endless.

The knob is cool. It always is.

She pushes the door open.

The den exhales at her. The television's static spills across the walls, painting them silver and blue. Dust hangs in the air like tiny stars, visible only when the light stutters. A glass sits on the coffee table beside a bottle, condensation pooling beneath it. The lamp in the corner buzzes once, too bright, then dims.

"Dad?"

Her voice trembles now with a rehearsed kind of dread.

The shape on the couch is exactly where it should be: one arm limp toward the floor, the other folded against a chest that doesn't rise. The head is turned away. The shirt is wrinkled. The fabric of the couch has darkened beneath him.

Heather's breath catches. This is where it always catches.

She doesn't move closer yet. She waits for the moment when

the bottle starts to fall.

And there it is.

It tips slowly, wobbling, balancing in defiance for one long second before gravity claims it. It rolls, the hollow clink barely audible under the television's hiss. It moves toward her foot with eerie precision, the same small arc it's made every single time she's dreamt this.

She crouches automatically, hands outstretched, whispering "No, no — please stop," though she knows it won't. It never does. The bottle makes contact with her toes, rocks once, and settles.

The whiskey has spilled out this time, seeping into the carpet, spreading toward the couch leg. The scent is strong now; raw and chemical. It burns her eyes.

She looks at the spill and whispers, "I'm sorry," though she doesn't know why.

The static falters. Just once. A hiccup in the signal. Then resumes, louder.

Heather rises.

Her legs feel too heavy for her body. She takes one step, then another, into the warm, stale air of the den. Each breath feels borrowed. The TV's glow flickers over her father's arm. There's a faint stain on his sleeve, something dark, rust-colored. Not fresh. Her gaze drags upward, but the light refuses to reveal what she needs to see. It never does.

On the end table: a photograph facedown. The frame's corner catches the static light, blinking like an eye. She already knows what's underneath it, but her fingers itch anyway. She reaches for it.

The frame feels cold, heavier than she expects. The moment she flips it over, the image burns through her — her parents beneath a canopy of orange leaves. Her mother's hair catching the sunlight. Her father's smile crooked, but soft. And two girls at their knees, both red-haired, both caught mid-laughter.

She drops the frame. The glass cracks, landing facedown again.

Heather's pulse hums louder than the television. She steps back, her heel brushing the bottle. It clinks softly. She looks down. For half a second, she thinks she sees something gleam inside it, but when she blinks, it's only the reflection of the TV.

Her breathing quickens.

From somewhere behind her, a faint sound — wood shifting, house settling, or something else. But not yet. The dream doesn't allow variations. Not yet. She swallows and forces herself to whisper again, "Dad?"

It dissolves. The static grows louder, filling the spaces the silence left behind. She watches the light from the TV tremble against his face, almost enough to make it seem like he might move, like his lips might part to answer her. She tells herself not to blink, but she does anyway.

The room is unchanged when her eyes open again. It always is.

Her legs fold. She sinks to the floor, cross-legged, palms pressing flat against the carpet. The fibers are damp and sticky beneath her hands. The smell is stronger here. She breathes through her mouth.

"This isn't real," she whispers. "You're not real."

The static softens, as though listening.

Her eyes drop to the edge of the couch. A dark shape dangles just beyond it, shadowed from the TV's flicker. She can't tell where the shadow ends and his hand begins. Her vision tunnels. The hum of the screen seems to slow.

And then she hears it.

Drip.

A single note, small and wet, falling from somewhere she can't see.

Drip.

Again, closer this time. It takes her a second to realize it's not coming from the ceiling or the sink. It's hitting the carpet. A dark patch growing wider near the couch leg, spreading into the fibers like ink.

Drip.

The sound syncs with her pulse. With each beat, it falls.

Drip.

The television flickers, bright white, and she sees it. The thread of red running down from his fingers.

Her breath locks in her chest.

Drip.

Her throat tightens. She wants to stand, but her knees refuse. The carpet feels like it's gripping her, holding her in place. The air thickens with iron and static.

Drip.

And then…

Stillness.

The sound cuts. The room holds its breath. Even the TV hums quieter, its glow fading to a dim blue haze. Heather stares into it, unblinking.

Her voice is small. Tired. Practiced. "Dad?"

Chapter 7

Memory didn't wait for her to wake up.

It was already there when her eyes opened — the den, the static, the way the bottle rolled with such ugly precision. It all hovered just behind her pupils like an afterimage burned into glass.

Heather lay still, listening. No drip this time. No TV. Just the soft tick of the vent in the corner and the whisper of fabric when she breathed.

The bed dipped a little under her weight, the mattress tracing the outline of how she'd slept. The sheets were still creased where he'd been, but the warmth was gone. Her hand drifted to that hollow automatically, fingers resting in the shallow dent his body had left. Maybe if she stayed like that long enough, her skin would remember the heat.

It didn't.

The room felt emptier than it had last night. She sat up, hair sticking to the back of her neck. The air carried a faint iron tang that made her hesitate before fading back into the sharper scent of detergent and old paper.

The chair was still by the window, her shoes lined up near the door, the small stack of folded clothes on the chair back exactly where she'd left them, but something had shifted. No eucalyptus. No trace of the Thai food. No Ben.

Had he said goodbye? She searched for the memory and found only weight, the heaviness that comes right before sleep, and the press of his hand on her waist. Nothing after that. Just the dream.

Her fingers curled against the sheet. "It was just a dream," she whispered, as if the room had asked. "The same one."

Her throat was dry. She pushed herself upright, the blanket sliding into her lap, and blinked against the early light pressing thinly through the blinds. Outside, clouds moved in slow, low sheets that dragged their bellies close to the ground. The glass was fogged in the corners where cold met the thin breath of the room.

On the desk, the folded paper waited exactly where she'd left it, a small, stubborn square against the wood. She swung her legs over the edge of the bed and stood, the floor cool beneath her bare feet. Her ankle twinged with the ghost of last night's tension; she ignored it.

She crossed to the desk. She just looked at the page, as if expecting it to have changed overnight. It hadn't. Same creases. Same faint impression of the ink inside, a barely visible ridge where she'd pressed too hard with the pen.

She picked it up, feeling the weight, thinking how silly it was that something so light could feel so much like an anchor. Her thumb traced the top fold, smoothing it, then refolding it along the same line. Preparation, more than anything. A way of telling herself she still had control over some things.

You can add more, she thought. Later. When you can breathe.

The thought comforted her more than it should have. She folded the paper again, once more, a smaller square now, and slipped it into her pocket. It settled against her leg, familiar.

She dressed slowly. Jeans, soft from wear. A long-sleeved shirt that still smelled faintly like the detergent she used; sharp and clean, clinical in a way that made her teeth ache. She tugged her sleeves down over her wrists and rolled them once, a compromise between coverage and comfort.

Her hair was a tangled mess from the night before. She dragged a brush through it half-heartedly, caught sight of herself in the small mirror over the dresser, and looked away before she could do more than register pale skin, dark-ringed eyes, and hair that was too bright for this washed-out room.

Ben must already be up. He always was, moving through the building in those early hours before the rest of the world noticed morning had happened. He had mentioned the conference, the schedule, the scramble.

He was leaving tomorrow.

That was all.

That wasn't long.

Or it was forever.

She couldn't decide.

"Bring him coffee," she told herself. "Something normal."

She slipped her shoes on and opened the door.

The corridor greeted her with the low, steady hum of the building. Lights in the ceiling glowed a muted yellow.

Heather closed her door carefully until the latch clicked into place. The sound was oddly final. She tested the knob; it didn't move. Good. She didn't know why she needed proof, but she always checked.

She moved down the hallway with that morning hesitancy, each step measured at first, then loosening as the familiarity of the place wrapped around her like a worn-out sweater.

Voices filtered from behind one of the closed doors, and a radio murmured from another. The world had started without her.

At the end of the corridor, near the set of double doors that led out toward the courtyard, the coffee cart waited.

Today, the sign clipped to its handle said:

TODAY: COFFEE ~ TEA ~ MUFFINS

Underneath, in the same looping hand she'd seen before, someone had written:

rain or shine

It made something in her chest pinch. Her mother used to say that about school days, about trips — *We go, rain or shine.* They'd gone to the funeral, too. Rain or shine, kiddo.

A woman stood behind the cart, fiddling with a stack of lids. Heather recognized the shape of her, if not the exact details. Last time, she'd worn a forest-green cardigan. Today it was navy blue.

"Morning," the woman greeted, offering a small, practiced smile. "You're up early."

"Couldn't sleep," Heather answered. It was almost true. "Thought I'd grab some coffee."

"Good day for it," the woman replied, nodding toward the glass doors. Beyond them, the courtyard sat under a sky the color of dishwater, the air thick and waiting. Drops of moisture clung to the ivy on the walls, but they hadn't committed to falling yet. "Supposed to rain," she added. "Keeps threatening."

"Feels like everything's threatening," Heather muttered, mostly to herself. Then louder, "Two, please."

The woman's hands moved with easy efficiency, grabbing two paper cups and setting them under the silver spout. Coffee flowed in a dark, steady stream, steam curling up in small ghosts that vanished as quickly as they formed.

"How do you take it?" the woman asked, already reaching for sugar packets.

"One black," Heather answered. "One with… two sugars, no cream."

"Him?" The question carried no judgment, just curiosity.

Heather hesitated, then nodded. "Yeah."

The woman's smile nudged up at one corner. "Thought so." She tore open two sugar packets and tipped them neatly into the second cup, stirring with a small wooden stick. "Saw you two out there the other day," she added. "Nice to see people using the courtyard."

Nice. Using. They were oddly clinical, but Heather let them pass.

As the woman secured the lids, Heather's eyes drifted to the little basket of muffins on the lower shelf. Each one sat in its own crinkled paper wrapper, tops domed and cracked. Blueberry, maybe. Or some generic berry that looked like happiness and tasted like sugar and dye.

"Can I grab one of those, too?" she asked.

"Help yourself." The woman stepped aside. "Blueberry. Or that's what the box said."

Heather picked one, testing the weight of it in her hand. It was warm near the top, still holding onto the oven's generosity. She imagined handing it to Ben like it was nothing. Like she hadn't spent the last ten minutes rehearsing it in her head.

Coffee in one hand, muffin in the other, she realized she needed a third hand. "Do you — uh — have napkins?" she asked.

"Always." The woman plucked a small stack from a dispenser and held it out. "You want a carrier?"

Heather laughed, a small, self-conscious huff. "That might be smart."

The woman shifted, rummaging beneath the cart, and came up with a shallow cardboard drink carrier. Heather nested the cups into it carefully, set the muffin on top, and tucked the napkins between.

"There." The woman dusted her palms off on her cardigan. "All set."

"Thanks," Heather said.

The automatic doors beside them sighed open.

Cold air slid in, stroking her ankles through her jeans. Heather glanced toward the entry without thinking, expecting someone to step through, but no one came.

The reflection in the glass door doubled for half a second, showing two baristas, both moving slightly out of sync. Heather blinked, and the second one vanished, leaving only the one adjusting the stack of lids.

Her pulse lagged a beat behind her breath.

The doors yawned open to the courtyard, then closed again with a soft hiss. The motion sensor light above them blinked twice, as if confused.

A small line formed between the woman's brows. "Touchy today," she murmured to the mechanism, then looked back at Heather. "You okay?"

"Fine," Heather lied. Her fingers tightened around the cardboard carrier until it flexed. "Thanks for the coffee."

"Anytime," the barista replied, already reaching for the next stack of cups. "Rain or shine."

Rain or shine.

The words chased her into the hallway.

The building's temperature shifted noticeably the farther she moved from the courtyard.

Heather kept the carrier level, listening to the soft slosh of the coffee with each step. The folded paper pressed against her thigh like a small, insistent reminder of something she should remember but didn't want to turn over just yet.

Ben's office was in the next hallway over, near a set of stairs she'd started taking instead of the elevator. "Good for circulation," he joked once, clapping a hand to his chest. "We all need an excuse to move more."

She headed that way now, her mind already half in his office, imagining the way his face would change when he saw her. The surprise, then the half-smile. Maybe a comment about her timing, about how she'd saved him from bad vending machine coffee.

Maybe nothing. Maybe *you didn't have to.*

In her head, it went well. In her chest, something fluttered nervously anyway.

At the turn where her hallway intersected the next, she slowed. The lights here were a little dimmer. The white walls had a faint gray tint, like they'd been washed too many times.

She shifted the carrier to her left hand, flexing the fingers of her right. They tingled from gripping the cardboard too hard. She shook them out once, then rounded the corner.

And saw him.

Or it.

A figure at the far end of the corridor, where the hall met another, stood near the fire door. Tall enough to look wrong in that space. Shoulders wrapped in a dark hoodie, hood up, head bowed. The fabric looked damp, clinging in places, like it had soaked up the morning.

Heather's feet kept moving, but something in her slowed.

Her heart made a small, startled detour in her chest.

It's nothing, she told herself.

A patient or visitor.

Just a jacket and a person. That's all.

The figure didn't move. Didn't turn.

He just stood there, his weight slightly leaning toward the door like they were waiting for someone.

Heather's throat tightened. Each step forward sounded too loud in her ears, but the corridor swallowed the sound. She adjusted her grip on the carrier, the cups knocking gently against their cardboard slots. The muffin shifted on top, crinkling its wrapper.

She would have to either pass him or take the elevator. Turning around meant admitting to something, though she wasn't sure what.

Closer now. Ten yards.

Eight.

Six.

The figure didn't look up. No phone in the hand, no clipboard, no ID badge glinting on their chest. No small reassuring details to latch onto.

"Excuse me," she said, because the silence was worse. Her voice sounded thin, like it had taken a wrong hallway and ended up here by mistake. "Sorry, I just —"

No response.

Her skin crawled. She shifted closer to the opposite wall, letting the rough texture of the paint brush her sleeve. She held the carrier slightly away from her body to keep from bumping him.

A part of her brain chided her, *"You're being ridiculous, "* and another part hissed, *"Keep your distance."*

As she passed, the figure's head turned just a fraction. Not enough to show a face, but enough to know that motion was for her.

She didn't see his eyes or any features at all. The shadow of the hood was too deep. But the shift was there, like the air in the corridor had realigned around that tiny motion.

The smell hit her then. Damp fabric, metallic tang, something sour underneath. It snagged on memory. For the barest second, she was back in the den, with the faint copper taste in the air.

She almost dropped the coffee.

Her fingers spasmed, the cardboard carrier dipping dangerously. The lids thumped. A thin line of heat licked over the back of her hand where a drop escaped, and she gasped more at the familiarity of the sensation than the burn.

She walked faster. Didn't look at him again.

Eyes on the scuffed floor tiles and the curls of steam escaping from the coffee lids.

Just turn into the stairwell. Just go.

She reached the door and pushed it open with her shoulder. The cool, echoing stairwell swallowed her whole, and she was suddenly aware of how foolish it was. Her shoulder sagged; she let out a shaky laugh she didn't entirely trust.

"You're fine," she muttered. "You're fine, it's —"

She risked one glance back through the small wired window in the stairwell door.

The corridor beyond was empty.

No hoodie. No tall shadow. No damp fabric smell.

Just the hallway, quiet and empty.

Heather stared for a beat too long, the edges of the world smearing slightly at the corners of her vision.

Nothing.

That was worse than if he'd still been there.

She swallowed, pulled the door shut until the latch clicked, and turned to face the stairs.

The folded paper in her pocket creased against her thigh when she moved, like a tiny heartbeat that hadn't decided which direction to beat in yet.

The stairwell smelled faintly of dust and old paint, that mix of neglect and cleanliness that came from mopping over the same grime a hundred times. The lights hummed with a sound too thin to be called comfort.

Heather steadied the cardboard carrier against her chest and took the first step up. The echo of her footsteps rose and folded over itself in soft, wrong rhythms.

You're fine.

You're fine.

Halfway up, a small draft touched the back of her neck. The stairwell exhaled a pocket of colder air from below.

She looked down.

The light fixture on the landing below flickered once. Twice. Then steadied.

She exhaled a laugh that didn't sound like her own and kept going. The second flight creaked, not because concrete should creak, but because her brain needed the sound to match the fear in her body.

The paper cups rattled softly in the tray.

She focused on the motion.

One step, two, shift weight, don't think.

Until she heard it.

Another step.

Behind her.

Heather froze.

Her throat clenched, the air in it turning sharp. She twisted slightly, just enough to glance up the stairwell. Nothing. The narrow flight she'd already climbed was empty.

But she could swear she'd heard a shoe drag.

Her pulse thumped so hard it made the edges of her vision shiver.

"It's nothing," she whispered, but the whisper had a tremor. "It's just echoes."

The stairwell listened.

Then answered.

One tap from above.

Something, someone, moving.

Heather took a step up, faster this time. Her elbow brushed the metal rail. Cold. Sticky. Sweaty.

The air below her changed.

Her body knew before her brain did.

She broke into motion, one hand gripping the rail, the other balancing the carrier like it was proof she could still pretend to be normal. The cups sloshed, hot liquid threatening to spill over.

The stairwell groaned.

She didn't look back.

Not until she reached the last flight.

When she did, she caught it again: a figure, a blur of dark fabric, a hood angled just enough to catch the light.

They were closer now.

Too close.

Heather's toe caught the edge of a step. The carrier tipped, cups wobbling. One lid popped off, splattering coffee up her sleeve.

She gasped, tried to grab it, and the world tilted.

For a suspended instant, gravity disappeared. Just air and sound, and the violent pulse of *no no no* —

Then the drop.

Her shoulders hit first. Then her hips. The coffee went up, spinning in an arc that spattered across the wall like ink.

The sound was small.

It didn't even feel like falling until she hit.

Her elbow clipped the next step, then her knees, and then she was at the bottom, her back pressed against the landing, lungs locked in a scream that wouldn't come.

The carrier lay crushed beside her; both cups on their sides. A slow brown bloom spread across the floor, seeping into the cracks.

Heather's breath came back in shallow, panicked bursts. Her wrist burned. Her arm, she couldn't tell where the sting began and ended as it pulsed with something hot.

She sat up, or tried to. The motion made the world tilt again. Her right arm screamed as she lifted it, and the sleeve clung to her skin in damp, red patches.

Blood.

Not much, but enough. It glimmered in a thin line where the sleeve had torn open.

She blinked through the shock and found the source: a screw jutting from the railing post, the head dark with rust.

The metal was slick with her blood now.

A disbelieving laugh broke from her chest, "Of course." She pressed her fingers over the cut. "Of course it's rusted."

Coffee and iron filled the air, sweet and metallic. The smell was dizzying.

She pulled herself up, legs shaking, and pressed her back to the wall. The stairwell behind her loomed quiet, light humming like insects.

Empty.

Her heart refused to believe it.

No one there.

No footsteps.

No dark fabric.

Just the walls and her own breath, coming too fast.

She took a step toward the door at the landing above, the one that led to Ben's office. Her blood left tiny crescent marks on the rail where she steadied herself.

The folded paper crinkled in her pocket as she moved, sticking slightly to her thigh. She clutched it through the fabric without knowing why.

The door waited ahead, painted a dull institutional blue. The small glass window near the top showed nothing but the blue of a hallway beyond.

Her fingers slipped once on the handle before she got a grip. She pushed it open with her shoulder.

The hallway on the other side looked wrong, as if it had been redrawn in a hurry; the angles were too sharp and the lights too white.

Heather blinked hard until the edges softened.

An employee at the far end didn't glance her way. A phone rang somewhere distant.

Her arm throbbed. The warmth of the blood had turned tacky, cooling in thin, sticky rivers beneath her sleeve. She pressed her hand over it again and felt the pulse against her palm.

Ben's office door was halfway down the hall, the wood grain darkened from years of handling. She focused on it like a lifeline.

Her steps were uneven, the sound of her shoes mismatched against the tile. The echo bounced, lasting forever.

When she reached the door, she didn't knock. She pushed it open with the same urgency she'd used on the stairwell door, as if something were still behind her.

He was there.

He sat at his desk, chair angled toward the window, light slicing across his face. Papers were spread across the surface behind him, a pen resting loosely between his fingers as if he'd paused mid-thought.

The moment he saw her, he stood so fast the chair rolled back and bumped the wall.

"Heather," his voice broke, caught halfway between relief and reprimand. He crossed to her in two strides. "What happened?"

"I fell," she breathed. "It's fine. It's not —"

Her words tangled when he reached for her arm. She tried to pull it back out of reflex, but he already had her wrist in his hand, turning it gently toward the light.

The tear in her sleeve pulled wider. The cut wasn't deep, but it looked angry. The skin split, dark line rimmed with rust-colored streaks.

Ben's jaw tightened. "You should've told someone."

"I didn't —"

He didn't let her finish. He moved toward the cabinet against the wall, already pulling open drawers. The sound of bottles and boxes clinking filled the silence.

Heather hovered near the door, dizzy from both blood loss and adrenaline. The smell of antiseptic drifted toward her even before he uncapped anything.

"Sit," he said, gesturing to the chair by the small side table. The tone wasn't unkind, but it left no room for argument.

She obeyed.

The world narrowed to the small circle of his hands; the movement of cotton against her skin, the sting of alcohol that made her flinch.

"Sorry," he murmured automatically, though his focus never wavered.

The sharp scent flooded her nose, clean and chemical. She tried to breathe around it, but it filled every space.

His breath brushed her wrist as he worked. The nearness should have comforted her; instead, it pinned her in place.

He worked efficiently. The pad of his thumb brushed against her wrist once as he adjusted the gauze, and the touch sent a current through her, unwanted and electric.

"Does this hurt?"

"No."

"Liar," he said quietly, not as an accusation, but as fact. He taped the bandage down, smoothing the edge with two fingers.

When he looked up, his expression softened. "You're shaking."

"I'm fine."

"Heather." Her name was both a warning and a concern. "You're pale. Sit still for a second."

Ben turned back to the desk and opened the top drawer, allowing the small click to break the silence. She watched as he pulled out a narrow white envelope.

Unmarked and neat, like it had been waiting there for her.

He turned it once between his fingers before extending it across the desk. "Here," he said softly.

"It's just something mild. You've barely slept."

He hesitated, then added, "You don't have to take it. Just... have it if you need it."

Her gaze lingered on the envelope. "What is it?"

"Nothing strong," he assured. "You'll feel better in the morning."

The envelope rested in her lap. "You think this is about that?"

He exhaled, leaning against the desk. "Everything's about that right now. You're exhausted."

Her hand twitched in her lap. "Someone was in the hallway," she said.

He blinked once. "Who?"

"I don't know." It came out faster than she meant it to. "A man. A hoodie. He was just... there."

Ben's face didn't change, but something behind his eyes cooled. "It might've been someone passing through."

"No." She shook her head as the heat rose in her chest. "He was following me. I heard him on the stairs — I know I did."

Ben glanced toward the door, as if he was considering it.

Then he crouched in front of her, voice low.

"Heather. You fell. You hit your head. Your mind can fill in gaps when it's scared."

He placed his hand over hers.

"That can happen. Especially when you already feel on edge."

His tone was soothing.

Practiced.

She was already nodding before she decided to. "Maybe," she said.

He stood again, stepping back, giving her space that was somehow still too close. "Go rest. No more stairs today."

"I can walk myself."

"I didn't ask if you could."

Something about the sentence made her breath hitch.

He must have noticed. His next words were softer. "You're

safe here."

It should have comforted her, but it didn't.

Ben offered her the paper cup from his desk; water, clear and harmless.

"Drink," he eyed, and she did.

When she looked up, he was watching her.

"I'll check on you later." The way he said it left no room for argument.

She stood, her legs uncertain but functional. "It's okay," she murmured, more to herself than him. "I can do it."

He nodded once, slowly. "Then do."

She left before she could change her mind with the white envelope trembling in her hand.

Chapter 8

And the room had that late-afternoon hush that softens every sound into fabric. The radiator ticked and then forgot what it was doing. Outside, the light thinned to a gray overcast. Her sleeve stuck to her forearm where the bandage ended and the fabric began; when she peeled it back a little to look, the gauze held a faint pink map of the day.

On the desk, next to the lamp with its warm oval of light, lay two things that hadn't moved since morning: the narrow white envelope he'd pressed into her hand, and the square of folded paper she kept making smaller when the world felt too large. She pushed the envelope farther from her without thinking, as if distance could dilute it. The folded page she slid closer until it touched her knuckle.

She rubbed her thumb over the top crease of the square, smoothing what she'd already smoothed ten times.

A clean sheet waited to the right of the lamp. She pulled it into the light. The pen was where she left it; she clicked it once and flinched at the sound, then put the tip to the corner and didn't write for ten slow breaths.

The bandage tugged when she leaned forward.

Dear Dad,

The D felt too sharp. She let the pen go softer.

I don't know how to start without going back, and it hurts to go back, and I keep going back anyway. I keep writing to prove you existed.

She paused. The words didn't look like much on the bare page, but they were already so heavy.

Today I tried to do something normal. I brought coffee. I thought if I handed someone a paper cup and said, "Here," the world would be less slippery for the length of one sip. It wasn't. I fell on the stairs. There was a loose screw, and I met it with my arm. You'd have laughed and then brought your whole toolbox like it was a personal insult.

She smiled because it was true. The memory of him crouched under a sink with a flashlight, swearing softly at a washer that refused to be more washer than rust. A little human miracle to fix what never wanted to be fixed.

I saw someone in the hallway before that. He stood as still as a coat on a hanger. He didn't say anything, and I told myself that meant he didn't exist. Later, when I heard steps, I decided those were mine. This is what I keep doing: naming things until they lose their teeth.

The pen left a darker dot where she'd paused too long. She smoothed the page with the side of her hand, as if that might even the ink.

They reopened the case. Did you hear me, Dad? The Autumn Murders. Everyone says it like a season you can opt out of by changing your calendar. I don't know why that phrase makes my skin feel too tight.

The lamp hummed. She wrote slower.

Mom's photo is still in my head. I keep thinking about the day in the yard with the leaves. Copper and red, and that smell you only get once a year, when the air is cold but not cruel. You had your hand on both our shoulders. Sometimes I think we were the weight you liked best.

I dreamed of you last night. The same way as always. TV snow. Bottle. The sound you don't want to put a name to. I did all the usual things. It's almost a relief now, the routine of it. A safe nightmare. Isn't that a ridiculous sentence?

She put the pen down for a second and pressed her thumb and forefinger to her eyes until the lights sparked. When she looked again, the letters had sharpened, black riding lightly over white.

I keep wanting to tell you the parts that make me look better. That I'm brave. That I didn't run. But I keep dissolving, Dad. I keep becoming steam around the edges, and I wanted you to see me solid at least once.

She let that stay. The page wanted more.

Sometimes I think forgiveness is a room with no chairs. You have to stand and decide to stay. I don't know where to put the part of me that still wants you to be the version in our family picture. What do I do with the hand that tips the bottle? What do I do with the way the house remembers your voice without your laughter? I keep writing to prove you existed, and then I have to pick which one of you existed harder.

The radiator ticked twice, then was done. She shifted in the chair, and the bandage tugged.

He wrapped it. He was careful. He gave me an envelope I haven't opened. He said I'm safe, which made my throat go tight. I want to believe him. I want to believe someone. This is getting pathetic, right? Don't answer that.

She blew on the ink as if that might set it faster.

I should tell you something kind, so this isn't just a ledger. Here: I remembered the way you cut the crust off my sandwiches without making a fuss about it. I remembered the time I scraped my knees on the sidewalk and you said, "That's how you know they work." I remembered the dictionary you bought from a yard sale because it had "good heft," and then you pressed my hand to the cover and said, "Learn the texture of things."

She lifted her hand from the paper and pressed her palm to the desktop, as if to check whether texture could travel through years.

I'm learning it. The texture of grief. It's not smooth or sharp. It's that middle ground where skin can't decide whether to toughen or split. I want you to be forgiven. I want to be forgiven for all the times I point my anger at the wrong wall. I want to stop counting the drip in my sleep. I want to forget the exact sound of glass against wood. I don't know if I want to stop dreaming you.

The pen skipped. She looped back over a letter to fill it.

Holly and I are not good at the part where sisters just... talk. We do the arithmetic of each other. What was owed. What was paid. I think we both keep looking for someone to grade us mercifully. You were supposed to be that person. That isn't fair. It also might be true.

She let the pen rest. The top of her back ached from leaning toward the desk too long.

I'm going to fold this and not send it, because there is nowhere to send it and because sending isn't the point. The point is putting your name on a line and not flinching. I keep writing to prove you existed. Maybe I keep writing to prove I do too.

Love,

H

She watched the ink dry on the H, as if it might change its mind. It didn't. She sat back and shook out her hand. The bandage itched; she pressed the clean edge of her sleeve down over it.

The envelope on the desk had inched closer somehow, or maybe the lamp's glow made it look that way. She slid the letter aside and set the envelope beside it. The two whites matched, seamless.

She folded the letter once. The crease sounded louder than it should have. She folded it again, smaller, the way she always did, to allow control to shape in her hands. She set it on top of the other square, palm over both, feeling the paper's cool through her skin. If anyone had opened the door just then, they might have thought she was keeping a secret from the table itself.

From somewhere in the vent, air shifted. The room cooled, then warmed, just enough to make the hair on her arms notice. Heather sighed and closed her eyes.

You always come back, she thought, and didn't know if she meant the dream or the letter or the ache.

A sound threaded the quiet.

"*Bug*," someone whispered.

She sat up. Her hand landed on the paper with more force than she meant. The lamp did not move. The room did not darken, and no one stood by the door. She listened until listening itself had its own pulse.

"*Bug*," the voice repeated, softer, patient, as if the speaker had all the time in the world to wait for her to recognize it.

She looked at the vent. She looked at the corner where the shadow of the dresser made another shadow inside itself. She looked at the reflection out the window and saw only the lamp, the corner of her shoulder, and the small square of paper under her hand.

"Dad?" It left her before she knew she'd chosen it.

The whisper didn't come again. The room exhaled the way rooms do when they decide they're not complicit.

Heather slid both papers into the top drawer and closed it carefully, avoiding the urge to check and recheck. She left the envelope on the desk. She turned the lamp down one click.

She sat for one more minute, hands empty, and let the minute be what it was. Then she stood, causing her sleeve to catch the bandage again.

On the way to the bed, she paused at the vent. She did not say anything to it, but pressed her fingers to the metal grille and felt nothing but the faintest breath of warm air moving past her skin.

"Rain or shine."

The sentence didn't mean anything useful, but somehow it helped.

Chapter 9

Fear had gotten subtle over the years.

Heather stood in the hallway, one hand wrapped around the receiver, the coiled cord brushing her wrist like a vein outside her skin. The fluorescent bulb above her hummed with a thin, headache-colored light.

The receiver was heavy in her palm, familiar in a way that made her uneasy. She tried to keep her bandaged arm still, but the moment her wrist flexed, the gauze tugged, reminding her that even small movements could hurt.

Call her.

The thought had been circling since she capped the pen on the letter. It had woven itself through the whisper in the vent, through the scrape of the dresser drawer, through the way the light outside refused to commit to either brightness or gloom.

Call her.

She had tried not to listen. But the word Holly had kept drifting to the surface of her mind like something that refused to stay drowned.

Now the dial tone buzzed in her ear, flat and patient. She knew the number by muscle memory; her fingers had dialed it so many times that the pattern lived somewhere in her wrist bones.

One ring.

Two.

Three.

By the fourth ring, she'd hang up. A small mercy for both of them.

"Hello?" Breathless, hurried.

Heather's fingers clenched around the cord. "Hey."

"Hang on," Holly's voice blurred away from the receiver. "Abby, leotard on now, not in five minutes — no, not that one, the other one — sorry, hi, I'm here." A rustle, the sound of the phone changing hands. "Heather?"

She hadn't expected the tiny twist in her chest at hearing her name like that. "Yeah. It's me."

A pause, then a quick exhale. "You okay?"

It was the kind of question that had a right answer and a true answer, even though they were rarely the same.

"I'm… here," Heather said finally.

"Okay." Holly's voice softened a notch. "Good. That's good."

In the background, something clattered onto a hard floor. A child's voice protested. Holly covered the receiver, her scolding muffled but sharp. When she came back, her tone had a different edge, thinner, stretched.

"Sorry. They decided now was the perfect time to reenact a natural disaster in the kitchen."

Heather started at the scuffed toe of her shoe. "It's fine."

Another small pause. "How's your arm?" Holly asked.

Heather's stomach flickered.

She hadn't told her. Ben wouldn't have told her. No one should have known.

"I don't know — someone mentioned you'd gotten hurt. It doesn't matter." Holly exhaled. "Are you okay?"

"It's nothing," she said instead.

"I slipped on the stairs. Hit a screw that shouldn't have been there." She tried to make it sound ridiculous. "Occupational hazard of having limbs."

Holly made a low sound that might have been a laugh. "You always did find the one sharp corner in any room."

"Talent," Heather murmured.

Silence settled between them. Heather could hear the distant kitchen chaos, the squeak of a cupboard door, the thud of something being set down too hard, but the gap between their breaths widened.

"I, um…" Heather shifted the receiver from one ear to the other. The bandage brushed her shirt; she winced. "I wrote something today."

"Wrote?" Holly echoed.

Her thumb rubbed a little circle into the phone's plastic. "A letter."

"To whom?"

She hesitated, feeling foolish now that the thought was out in the air. "Dad."

The line went very quiet. Even the background rustling seemed to dim.

"Oh," Holly said at last. "Okay."

"I'm not sending it," Heather hurried to add, as if she needed to prove she wasn't the unhinged one.

"There's nowhere to send it. I just… needed to put his name at the top of something and not —" Her voice thinned. "And not look away."

Holly exhaled a breath that sounded like it had been kept in storage. "What did you say?"

"I don't know." Heather let out a shaky laugh. "Everything.

Nothing…that I keep dreaming of him. That I'm tired of only remembering the worst version of him… stuff like that."

"Right." A chair creaked faintly on Holly's end. "That sounds… good, actually. Hard, but good."

"Does it?" Heather traced the fraying edge of the bedspread with her bare toes. "Feels like scratching at a scab and calling it therapy."

"Sometimes that's half of therapy," Holly said. A spoon clinked against something. "How are your sessions with Dr. Powell going? Are they… helping?"

Heather stared at the small square window in the hallway door.

"They're fine," she huffed. "I actually have one later today."

"Oh." A small clatter, maybe a bowl being moved. "Well… that's good. You should go."

"Donna called me. Again." Holly clipped.

A familiar irritation flared in Heather's throat. "What did she want now? More 'patterns'? New ways to say 'Autumn Murders' like it's a brand?"

"She wanted clarification," Holly said. "I hung up."

"Good." The word came out more vicious than she intended.

"They're… saying a lot of things," Holly continued, slower now. "Online. In the comments. Mom would tell me not to read them. I keep reading them anyway."

"Of course you do," Heather muttered.

"I keep waiting for someone to say something that makes it less awful," Holly added, a humorless laugh catching at the edge of the sentence. "They haven't, in case you were wondering."

"I wasn't," Heather scoffed. "I don't want to know what they're saying."

"You say that," Holly replied quietly, "but you called me to talk about it."

They landed with a small, precise sting. Heather's throat tightened. "I called you because I wrote to him," she snapped. "Because after writing to a dead man, calling my living sister felt like the logical next step."

Silence again. Longer this time.

"Okay," Holly said, very soft. "Fair."

Heather sighed, pressing the heel of her hand briefly to her eyes. "Sorry. That was… I didn't mean —."

"No," Holly cut in. "You did. It's okay. Just… don't pretend you didn't."

Something weary in her tone that scraped Heather's nerves raw. "What's that supposed to mean?"

"It means," Holly said, voice flattening, "every time we talk about Dad, we end up in the same place. You poke at the parts I left behind, I poke at the parts you kept. We're very consistent."

"Holly," she began.

Holly inhaled sharply. "Heather, please don't start with —"

"I'm not starting anything."

"You are," Holly replied.

"I don't need anything."

"You called me."

Heather closed her eyes. Her throat tightened until the next breath had to be forced in.

"Forget it," she whispered.

"Heather —"

"Really. It's fine." She fell apart as she spoke them. "Same problem, right? Just new stakes."

The line went quiet.

Then Holly's voice returned, soft with something dangerously close to guilt. "I didn't mean it like that. I just… can we talk later? I'm trying, okay?"

Heather forced her voice steady. "Yeah. Sure. Later."

"Okay. I —"

Heather hung up before the sentence finished.

The click echoed down the hallway, louder than it should have been.

She stood there with the receiver still in her hand, staring at nothing. The cord hung from the phone like a loose tendon. Her pulse sat too close to the surface, like someone could read it just by watching her breathe.

She set the receiver back in its cradle. It settled with a soft plastic thud.

Her reflection in the hallway window wavered once, like the glass had blinked.

I have a meeting later.

She checked the clock on the wall.

Not time yet, but close enough.

Heather inhaled, held it until it burned, then let it out, slow. Her hand drifted toward her pocket, thumb brushing the folded square of paper inside.

She turned toward the hallway.

* * *

Dr. Powell didn't look up immediately.

Heather stepped into the office and closed the door behind her, the latch giving a soft, civilized click. The room was a shade too cool. Powell's pen moved steadily over a file, neat strokes, nothing hurried or emotional about them.

She stood there until he finished the sentence he was writing. Only then did he cap the pen, align it with the edge of the folder, and lift his gaze.

"Right on time," his voice had its usual calm neutrality.

Heather sat in the chair across from his desk. The cushion sighed. She rested her uninjured hand on her knee to keep it from trembling, then pretended that she wasn't doing exactly that.

"How's the cut?"

"Fine." She tugged her sleeve lower. "Barely anything."

His eyes flicked to her wrist. "It must've hurt."

"It's fine."

He clicked his pen and wrote something in the margin of his pad. The quiet scratch of ink filled the room more than her breathing did.

"Nightmares?" he asked.

"Same one," she admitted.

He nodded once, as if that answer fit somewhere on a chart. She hated how calm he was. How calm he always was.

Heather shifted in her chair. Her fingers brushed the folded square in her pocket.

He leaned back, studying her. That made it worse. The quiet in the room grew a spine.

"You've had a difficult few days," he said. "The interview. The case reopening. The dream."

She swallowed hard.

He watched her with that steady, clinical focus that was almost kind, if not for how precise it felt. "Tell me about your sister."

She didn't realize how much time had passed until the clock ticked louder in the silence.

Heather looked at her hands. "I talked to Holly."

"How did it go?"

She let out a humorless breath. "Pick any synonym for disaster."

Powell waited.

"She thought I was picking a fight," Heather said. "I wasn't. Or… I don't think I was. She said —" Her voice caught. "She said we always end up in the same place."

"And did that feel true?"

"I hate that it felt accurate."

He didn't write this time. He just watched her, expression unreadable behind the glasses.

"Family patterns can repeat even when we don't want them to," he replied. "Especially under stress."

"Everything feels like stress right now."

"Tell me about the stairs," he continued.

She stared at the floor. "I thought someone was following me."

"Thought?"

Her jaw clenched. "I saw someone, okay? A man. Hood up. Standing in the hall."

"What did he do?"

"He just… stood there." Her breath shook. "Then he moved. Or I did. Or — I don't know."

"Fear can make neutral moments feel like something else." Powell's pen hovered above the paper, then lowered again, "But we can't rule out that someone was there."

"So you think I imagined him."

"I think you felt unsafe," he said. "And when we feel unsafe, we fill silence with threat. It's a very human response."

She swallowed. "It doesn't feel human."

"It is." He closed the notepad softly. "You've had sleep disruption, emotional strain, resurfaced trauma, and now physical pain. It's natural for your perceptions to shift."

Heather's eyes burned. "I'm trying."

"I know." His tone stayed measured.

She looked at the small clock on the side table, its second hand ticking like footsteps.

Powell followed her gaze, then said, "Before we finish, my schedule shifts starting tomorrow. I'll be out for a couple of days, so we'll resume sessions on Sunday afternoon."

He folded his hands. "Heather, you're not alone in this. Even when it feels that way."

She didn't answer. Her throat couldn't decide how to work.

"You've done enough for today," Powell said gently. "Try to rest."

She stood. Her knees wobbled once before steadying.

At the door, that prickling sensation returned, the sense of being watched, and she couldn't quite trust the room behind her.

But she opened the door.

The hallway's window reflected her back at her, except the reflection hesitated a fraction of a second before matching her step.

She didn't look again.

Chapter 10

Twisted light filtered through the ivy, the courtyard breathing with a soft hush, like a library that had learned to love the sound of leaves. Morning light pooled on the flagstone in pale squares, and the ivy along the brick wall swayed as if nodding to an old song. Heather took a seat at a wrought-iron table near the oak, cupping a paper cup of juice between her palms.

A gray-haired man leaned on a walking stick while a younger woman read to him from a book. Two boys tossed crumbs to a pair of sparrows and laughed when the birds fought over a flake of crust. A barista rolled a rattling cart across the paving stones, little cups knocking gently against one another like tiny bones. The whole place had a low hum to it, gentle and contained, like a cafe that had forgotten the music but still remembered rhythm.

Heather set the cup down and pressed her fingertips to the table's cool lattice, tracing the rust-laced curves. She tried to count her breaths the way Ben liked her to. In for four, hold for four, out for six. His voice had a way of settling into her ribs when she remembered it. It helped, until it didn't.

A thin man with too-long sleeves paced near the far planter. He kept lifting his chin, scanning the tree line as if waiting for a signal, as if listening. Every seventh step, he turned and glanced back across the courtyard. The movement pulled at her nerves, an invisible thread that kept tugging and tugging.

She told herself not to stare, to focus on the cup and the way the juice held the light.

A shadow flickered at the edge of her vision. She tightened her grip. The oak trunk cast a bar of darkness across the path; the shape almost looked like a man's broad shoulder, a hood drawn up. Then a branch shifted, and it was only a slice of shade again.

You're fine, she told herself. People are around you. You are breathing. You are safe.

A chair scraped beside her. "Mind if I join?" a woman asked softly. She had kind eyes and an orange wristband that caught the light. Heather blinked at it and saw a pretty bracelet with a plastic shine. The woman sat, setting down a cup and a muffin wrapped in paper that read *Smithsdale* in faded ink. The letters looked like leaves fallen in a line.

"You come out here a lot." The woman offered.

"Sometimes," Heather said. "It's quiet. My apartment's just over that wall." She nodded toward the brick, though there was no visible door.

The woman's eyes flicked there, "Quiet is good."

The woman picked at her muffin, leaving crescents in the top where her fingers pressed. "Loud makes things shake loose."

Heather watched the birds. One had a missing feather near its throat. It dove and hopped, then dove again, undeterred. "Do you ever feel like... people are watching?" she asked before she could stop herself.

The woman's gaze lifted, thoughtful. "All the time." She smiled, not unkindly. "Usually it's just the wind, or the way shadows pretend to be something they're not."

Heather nodded, as if they had exchanged something valuable. Then she looked down and saw that her hands were trembling. The juice rippled, catching pieces of sky.

A cart rattled behind her. She flinched. The barista parked it near the door and began to hand out tiny cups, each with a cheerful white lid. Names were called in a careful voice that sounded like a lullaby smoothed with practice.

"Heather?" the voice asked, gentle and certain.

She turned. The barista smiled with her whole face, the kind of smile people used to coax skittish animals. "Your morning juice," the barista said and placed a second cup on the table, this one with a label stuck crooked along the side. The letter swam, then steadied into her name.

"Thank you," Heather murmured. She wanted to ask if she had seen the hooded man nearby; however, she kept the question in her throat where it was safer.

The thin man with too-long sleeves paused beside the oak. He stood very still, face tipped to the sun. Then he looked toward Heather as if he'd heard her thinking.

Not at her, she corrected herself. Past her. Over her shoulder.

She turned without moving her feet. The trellis blurred, the leaves meshed into netting, and beyond it the service road cut a dull line through the lawns. A groundskeeper pushed a bin, his shoulders hunched against the breeze. Not a threat, she told herself. Still, something in the angle of his cap prickled her skin. She watched him until he disappeared behind the hedge. When he was gone, she realized she'd been holding her breath.

"Are you waiting on someone?" the woman asked, voice softer than the rustle of ivy.

"Maybe," Heather said. "My sister. Or Ben." She tasted the name like a cherry dropped into water. It colored everything.

She could almost hear him, even, low, with the kind of tone that turned even questions into instructions. *When things settle, we might go somewhere.* She wanted to ask where, but he'd just smiled like the answer was meant to stay quiet.

"Sounds nice," the woman said, as if to a child promising to move to the moon. "The trick is, shadows follow. Even into nice places."

Heather looked down at her hands. The tremor had eased, but only because she'd clenched them. Across the courtyard, the boys had given up on the sparrows and were making a game of stepping on their own shadows, giggling when their feet landed on dark feet. One boy leaped and missed, and laughed harder. Their noise filled the space where a voice in her head usually lived.

A breeze moved through the oak. A few leaves let go and drifted down, landing in the grass with the softness of feathers. The air smelled faintly of bleach, and something sweet underneath it, like cherry cough syrup or melted candy.

Her teeth sank into her lip. She tasted metal. "Do you hear that?" she asked suddenly. The woman tilted her head.

"Hear what?"

"The humming." It was there, constant and low, as if the building itself was breathing. Refrigerators. Lights. Machines behind walls. She swallowed. "Never mind."

Ben would say, *Name three things you can see.* She tried. Ivy. Birds. A plastic cap sat abandoned on the path. *Two things you can feel.* The cup's warmth. The scrape of iron under her palm. *One thing you can hear.* Humming.

"Okay," she whispered, to no one and to him.

A sparrow leaped onto the table, bold as a thief, and pecked at the muffin wrapper. The woman laughed, a small, real sound. "Hey," she chided, and shooed it with two fingers. The bird jumped back and cocked its head as if offended, then darted away in a rust-brown blue.

Heather reached for her cup and knocked it with the back of her hand. It tipped, the lid popping askew, and red liquid streamed across the iron curls and down onto the stone. It spread quickly, a bright bloom that turned darker as it met the dust in the grooves. For one second, she wasn't in the courtyard; she was in her nightmare, blood drying against her skin, something dark and wet inching closer across the floor.

She jerked her feet back. The chair scraped a sharp, ugly sound that made three heads turn. "Sorry," she said, too loudly.

"It's just juice," the woman said softly. Her voice had no edges. "Happens all the time."

Just juice. Heather stared until the red dulled to a tired pink halo. The barista appeared beside them with a towel like a magician with a handkerchief. "No harm done," she said, and blotted the spill in quick, practiced circles.

"Thank you," Heather said. The barista nodded and rolled the towel into a neat rope and draped it over the cart's edge. The little cups jostled, lids chattering. The sound reminded Heather of teeth.

The chattering of the cups faded, but the clinking echoed in her mind. She blinked and looked up, and there he was again, motionless.

The man with the too-long sleeves stood against the brick now, as if he'd been waiting. He tilted his head like a dog hearing a distant whistle. Then, slowly, he lifted his hand upward, fingers aligning with the service road. Pointing. Or stretching. The gesture cut the air like a compass needle, aimed at something only he could see. A chill slid down Heather's spine, silent and sure as a blade laid flat.

"Do you need to go inside?" the woman asked, following Heather's gaze, though her eyes found only sunlight.

"I'm —" Heather started, and then again, quietly, "I'm fine." The words fit like a dress two sizes too small: squeezed in, zipped up, presentable if you didn't look too closely.

Heather stood. The chair wobbled and then settled. Her hands had stopped shaking, or she had simply learned to hold them in a way that hid it. She thanked the woman, though her voice sounded like it was traveling from somewhere far behind her.

At the door, she hesitated. Through the glass, her reflection floated, a pale double, layered over ivy and sun. The shimmer made her look like she belonged to both sides and neither.

A door.

A handle.

Her face.

The humming.

Names keep the world from unraveling.

She pushed through. Inside, the air was cooler, flatter, the hallway a straight line that didn't care how she felt. A cart clinked somewhere around the bend. Voices rose and folded over one another like sheets being shaken out. Heather didn't look back at the courtyard. She didn't need to. The feeling that had followed her all morning slipped in behind her like it had a right to.

You're fine, she told herself, pressing her palm to the wall as she walked. You are breathing. You are safe.

The hum inside the walls shifted just slightly.

She took one more step.
And that was when a voice behind her said, sharply:
"Heather?"
She froze.

Chapter 11

Everything in her tightened at once.

Heather turned, pulse stuttering.

Donna stood halfway down the hall, messenger bag slung across her chest, the camera strap wrapped so tightly around her wrist it looked like she'd been gripping it for miles. Her hair was wind-tossed, cheeks flushed from the morning air, eyes bright with the kind of determination that had nothing to do with kindness. It struck Heather that Donna hadn't just wandered in. She'd been looking for her. Maybe even waiting.

"Heather," Donna said again, softer now. "Can we talk?"

Heather's first instinct was to step back. Her second was to run. Neither reached her feet; her body simply locked.

"I… I'm busy," she said, brittle as frost.

"I won't take long." Donna took a slow, deliberate step forward. "I just have a few things I need to clarify for the article."

Article scraped something raw inside her.

"I already talked to you," Heather muttered. "And I said I didn't want to anymore."

"You did," Donna agreed, voice gentle but eyes too sharp, too awake. "But after the piece ran online yesterday, there were… reactions. Comments. Questions. People noticed patterns I missed the first time around."

Patterns.

Heather's stomach twisted.

Donna continued carefully, "Some readers think your father's timeline overlaps with—"

"No." Heather's voice cracked like a snapped branch. "We're not doing this."

Donna didn't flinch. She glanced briefly down the hall, as if making sure they were alone, then returned her gaze to Heather. "I'm not accusing him of anything. I'm trying to understand. There's a difference."

"No," Heather whispered. "There isn't."

Donna tried again, quieter. "When people read your interview... when you mentioned the noise you heard that night? The thing you said you'd never talked about publicly?" She hesitated. "People want to know what that meant."

Heather swallowed hard.

Voice in two rooms, same words, different man.

Donna's eyes dropped to the bandage on Heather's arm.

"You went tense during the interview," she said quietly. "And now you're hurt."

Heather shifted back a fraction. "It's nothing."

Donna shook her head, not unkindly, but with a journalist's precision. "Heather... are you okay? Really okay?"

"I said I'm fine."

"You don't look fine." Her voice had a new softness now—more apology than insistence. "I'm not trying to be the enemy here. I just—" she exhaled, "I worry when things line up like this. Old trauma, new injuries. People don't break all at once. They crack in patterns."

Pressure built behind her ribs. "What do you want?"

"To understand," Donna whispered. "That's all."

But the real question pushed up through the surface of her voice like a bruise:

What aren't you telling me?

"I need to go."

She stepped past Donna, pulse tightening, every instinct screaming to get away before something in her gave way. Donna didn't grab her, didn't call after her; she only watched with an expression Heather couldn't decipher, a crease between her brows that looked too much like concern.

Heather reached the corner of the hallway.

And froze.

The thin man lingered at the far end, unmoving and silent. He didn't turn towards her. Instead, his head tilted toward the wall, ear poised as if he were trying to catch whispers echoing from within the depths of the building.

Behind her, Donna's voice drifted, careful. "Heather? What is it?"

Heather swallowed. "Nothing."

She didn't wait for more. She turned sharply away from the far end of the hallway, resisting the pull to look again, and walked.

She didn't look back.

* * *

Heather shut the door behind her with more force than she meant. The click echoed in the small space, sharp as a knuckle cracking. She stood with her back pressed against the wood, trying to slow her breath and convince her ribs that nothing was trying to hunt her.

Something about the room was off.

Her eyes traced the familiar things first: the shelf with the old knick-knacks from her childhood, the thin strip of afternoon light cutting across the floor, the blanket still rumpled from where she'd sat writing yesterday.

All were still there, and hers, but something under it was rearranged.

Donna's questions clung to her skin like static.

And that look when Donna saw the bandage was concern, shaped like an accusation.

Heather rubbed her thumb over the gauze, then stopped when the tug stung.

She crossed the room slowly, resisting the urge to check the corners for movement she knew she wouldn't find. When she reached the bed, she sighed before sitting down.

She kept seeing the thin man at the end of the hall.

Still. Listening.

But the way he pressed his ear toward the wall had scraped something deep inside her, something that hadn't fully healed.

Heather shut her eyes, but that only made the memory clearer.

She opened her eyes again, staring at the far wall as if it might admit something.

She stood abruptly and crossed to the shelf, touching each object as if examining for any changes.

She placed the snow globe down carefully.

"I'm fine," she whispered to the room, as if saying it out loud could iron it into truth. "I'm okay."

Silence answered.

Then a faint shuffle from the hallway. Just another tenant, she told herself, although the thought was unconvincing.

She moved halfway, instinct pulling her toward the door. As she opened it, her gaze snagged on the phone.

Call him.

Just to hear his voice.

Just to steady the ground beneath her feet.

Heather's slow and shaky breath confirmed how much she needed the sound of someone she trusted.

The hallway closed in, thinner somehow. The light over the phone buzzed faintly, casting a cheap halo over the plastic cradle. The cord hung in a loose coil, half untwisted, like someone had left a thought unfinished there.

She stood in front of it and just… stared.

Her fingers were already lifting the receiver.

The dial tone hummed against her ear, steady and indifferent.

A soft clatter on the other end. Then his voice.

"Heather?"

The sound of her name in his mouth loosened something and tightened something else at the same time.

"Hey," she said, aiming for light and landing somewhere closer to frayed.

He sounded like he'd turned away from something. "I'm glad you called," Ben said. "I was going to try you later."

A faint murmur rose behind him. Clinking glassware. A chair scraping. Then, brief but clear, a woman's laugh, bright and close to the receiver, before fading.

Heather's fingers tightened on the cord.

"Am I… interrupting?" she asked.

"No," he said quickly. "I just stepped out of a session. There's a reception down the hall." He cleared his throat. "It's loud, that's all."

"You sound…" She searched for the right adjective and came

up empty. "Far away."

"That's because I am," he said, a tiny attempt at a joke. "Different city. Different bad hotel art on the walls."

Normally, that might've earned a smile, but it didn't this time.

"How are you?" he added. "Really?"

She swallowed. The question brushed too close to Donna's: *Are you okay? Really okay?*

"I'm fine," she said, because it was the script. Then, because it sounded hollow even to her, she added, "I just... needed to hear you."

His exhale crackled against the line. "I was thinking of you this morning," he said quietly. "How did the day go?"

She thought of the courtyard. The thin man with his ear to the wall. Donna, with eyes that were sharp and kind at the same time. The way the room was wrong when she came back.

"It was... weird," she whispered. "Donna found me."

A pause. "Donna."

"The reporter."

Another pause, slightly longer, like he'd turned the word over before answering. "What did she want?"

"To 'clarify a few things,'" Heather said, the quoted phrase sour on her tongue. "She said there were comments. People were noticing patterns. She said people think Dad's timeline overlaps with... with those murders."

Ben was quiet. She could almost see him pressing his fingers together, slotting words into neat rows before speaking.

"And how did that make you feel?" he asked.

She flinched. "Please don't do that."

"Do what?"

"Ask me like I'm in your office." Her voice came out too sharp. She softened it. "I called you. Not... him."

A small scrape sounded on his end. "I'm just trying to give you space to say what you need to say."

"I don't want space," she snapped softly. "I want you to react. I want you to say, 'That's awful, I'm sorry she cornered you, of course you're upset.' Not 'How does that make you feel?' I know how it makes me feel."

He let out a breath. When he spoke again, his tone was gentler. "Okay. You're right. I'm sorry. That's a lot to deal with, especially on top of everything else."

Some of the tension in her neck eased, just a fraction.

"I keep thinking about that night," she said, voice lowering. "And now Donna's poking holes in it like there's a right answer I haven't given her yet."

"She doesn't get the right answer," Ben said. "It's your memory. Your experience."

"She wants details," Heather went on. "She wants the sound cataloged and labeled. She wants to know what I heard and where I stood and how long the bottle rolled and whether our address lines up with her neat little headline."

"She wants a story," he replied. "That's not the same as wanting the truth."

"A murder story," Heather corrected quietly. "She wants to stitch my father into it like he was waiting for the right page."

Heather leaned her shoulder against the wall, letting the coolness soak through her shirt. "She said people don't break all at once. They crack in patterns."

On the other end, something rustled. "And what do you think about that?" he asked carefully.

"There you go again," she muttered. "You tell me."

Another pause. "I think you've been under more strain than anyone should be," he said. "Interview. Case reopened. Old trauma stirred up. And then you get hurt on the stairs." His voice tightened slightly on that last part. "It makes sense that everything feels sharper right now."

"You say that like it's a weather report," she replied.

"How would you like me to say it?"

"I don't know," she admitted. "Like you're not reading off a chart."

He was silent for a beat, then: "Heather... I'm not reading off anything."

He exhaled softly. "I stepped out into the hallway. It's the only place I could get a little quiet to talk to you."

She pictured it despite herself: him sitting with his back to a patterned wall, carpet ugly and loud under his shoes, suit jacket folded beside him. The image should have comforted her; instead, it made her chest ache.

"You didn't call yesterday," she said.

He blinked that she'd changed direction; she could hear it in the tiny lag before he answered. "I... tried," he said. "The line was busy, and then the evening got away from me. I'm sorry."

"Busy?" She stared at the phone cradle with sudden suspicion, as if it might confess. "I was there."

"You live in a building with other people," he reminded her gently. "Sometimes they use the phone too."

The logic was fine. It was still a lie, rubbed smooth enough to pass inspection.

"You said you'd check in," she murmured.

"I did check in," he replied, softer. "I asked about your arm. About your sleep. I'm talking to you now."

"That's not the same," she said. "You said you'd come back. That night. You said it in my room, and then I woke up alone, and everything smelled like detergent and old paper, and I didn't know if you'd been there or if I'd… dreamed it."

His breathing changed, barely. "Heather… when I said that, I meant emotionally."

Memory flickered like an unreliable film in a too-hot projector. The hallway. His voice. *You're pale. Sit still for a second.* The envelope. The water cup.

Had that not been checking in?

"I guess you're right," she murmured.

"That's okay," he said. "This is what happens when you're exhausted."

"Stop blaming exhaustion for everything," she snapped, sharper than she meant. "I'm tired, not incapable."

"I didn't say you were incapable."

"You think I exaggerated the man in the hallway," she pushed. "The hoodie. The sound on the stairs. You think I made that part bigger in my head."

"I think," he said slowly, "that you were scared. And fear reshapes things. It makes neutral shadows look like threats. It makes ordinary noises feel like footsteps following you."

"So you don't believe me."

"I believe you were afraid," he said. "I believe you felt followed. I also believe no one else saw him, and that the building was quiet after you fell."

She pressed the heel of her hand to her forehead. "That sounds like a very careful answer."

"I'm trying to be honest without feeding the fear," he said. "If I say, 'Yes, there was definitely a man stalking you,' how does that help you sleep tonight?"

"If there was," she whispered, "then I'd rather know it than have everyone pat my head and call it shadows."

"Heather."

The way he said her name, steady, low, was the same tone he used when she spiraled in his office. It made her both want to lean into it and shove it away.

"You misunderstand things when you're stressed," he said quietly. "Anyone would. That doesn't make you wrong. It just means your brain is trying to protect you in the only way it knows how."

"I'm not a malfunctioning alarm system," she said. "I know the difference between a feeling and a person."

"I know you do," he replied. "Most of the time."

That qualifier landed like a stone.

"Most of the time," she repeated.

"I'm not trying to insult you," he said. "I'm trying to name what's happening.

You've had more nightmares. You're jumpier. You've been reacting to things that aren't what they seem lately."

He let out a quiet breath.

"None of that is your fault. But it does mean your fear is very loud right now."

"And you're very far away," she whispered.

"I'm coming back Saturday," he reminded her. "We'll have time to go through everything properly. Not like this, with people milling around and an agenda breathing down my neck."

She heard a muffled announcement over a PA on his end—something about a breakout session, vague and distant.

"Of course, there's an agenda," she said. "There's always an agenda."

"Heather."

"You keep saying that," she went on, the dam creaking. "You keep saying we'll 'go through everything properly' and 'name what's happening' and 'structure will help.' You keep saying

I'm safe."

"Because you are," he said. "Where you are now—"

"Don't." The word came out sharper than intended. "Don't describe my life like a brochure."

He stopped. The silence on the line grew teeth.

"You are safe," he said again, slower, as if each word had been weighed. "Whatever else you feel, that part is true."

She stared at the far wall, at the faint hairline crack in the paint she'd never noticed before. It lodged in her throat, prickly.

"You keep saying that," she whispered. "Over and over. Like if you say it enough, it'll be real."

"It is real."

"It doesn't feel real," she snapped.

"What does it feel like?"

She laughed, a short, humorless sound. "Trapped."

His breath caught just audibly.

"You keep saying I'm safe," she said, the words forming on their own. "That's just another word for trapped."

It hung there between them.

When he finally spoke, his voice was softer. "That isn't what I mean when I say it."

"But it's what it feels like," she choked out. "You say 'safe,' but you're not the one standing on it. You're at some conference with bad coffee and laughing women."

He didn't defend himself right away. When he did, his tone had slid fully into that maddening, even register.

"I took this trip because it was scheduled months ago," he said. "Because if I keep my commitments, it means I'm dependable, including for you. If I cancel everything whenever things get hard, I stop being reliable and start being… reactive."

"You sound like a pamphlet again," she whispered.

"I'm trying not to make promises I can't keep," he said. "That's why I'm telling you exactly this: I will be back Saturday. I will see you on Sunday. We will talk without distractions. In the meantime, you're not alone in this, even when it feels like it."

The carefulness of it made her want to scream.

"I don't want 'people,'" she huffed. "I want you. Not you-with-your-professional-voice. You."

"I am me," he said. "Right now. Talking to you from a hallway instead of networking like I'm supposed to. That is not nothing."

It wasn't. That's the worst part.

Her throat ached. "I hate that I feel like I'm asking too much for wanting you to be here."

"You're not asking too much," he said. "You're asking the wrong thing at the wrong moment. I can't be in two places at once. That doesn't mean I've disappeared."

"It feels like you're fading," she whispered.

"Fear makes things look like they're fading when they're not," he replied. "Nothing has changed. You are safe."

It hit the same raw place. She squeezed her eyes shut.

"I shouldn't have called."

"Heather —"

"I thought it would help," her the words coming faster. "I thought hearing you would make things quieter. But you sound like a stranger in a hallway full of strangers, and suddenly I'm just another item on your list between panels."

"That's not fair."

"It's what it feels like."

A long, tired silence settled in. Somewhere on his end, a door opened and shut. A voice called something indistinct.

When he finally spoke, his voice was quieter than before.

"I care about you," he said. "Very much."

The sentence landed wrong. Too careful. Too placed.

"Yeah," she said hoarsely. "You care. Professionally. Structurally. Safely."

"That's not true," he gasped.

"Then stop sounding like it," she whispered.

"When I get back," he said finally, "we'll talk properly. Right now, I need you to do one thing: try to rest tonight. Let the other people around you carry some of this. You don't have to hold it all by yourself."

"Sure," she said. "I'll add 'rest' to my to-do list. Right under 'don't hallucinate men in hallways' and 'don't let reporters turn your life into content.'"

"Heather —"

She couldn't hear any more of that tone. That carefulness. That distance wrapped in concern.

"Have a good conference," she said, because the alternative was saying something that would shatter them both. "Enjoy the bad coffee."

"Heather, wait —"

She hung up.

The sound of the disconnect was oddly significant, resonating through the narrow hallway, ricocheting off the buzzing light above, and seeping beneath the door like a gentle stream.

She kept the receiver pressed against her ear, absorbing the silence on the other end.

Eventually, she lowered it into the cradle, where it settled with a soft, muted thud.

The hallway ahead seemed to stretch endlessly. Her reflection flickered faintly in the wire glass of the door, lingering for just a heartbeat before mirroring her movement.

"You're safe," she whispered.

Chapter 12

Leaving isn't an option. Not here.

The dream always starts the same.

The hallway stretches long and patient before her, the carpet thin from footsteps she doesn't remember taking. The air smells of damp wood and dust caught in fabric. Air that hasn't moved since that night. Her skin prickles, knowing exactly what comes next.

The light at the far end of the corridor blinks twice, steadying into a pale rectangle spilling from beneath the den door. The rest of the house sleeps. The hum of the refrigerator is gone. The clock has no tick. Only that light remains, pulsing faintly like a heart under gauze.

Heather stands barefoot, toes curling against the carpet's flattened threads. Her pajama hem brushes her ankles. Cotton, blue, thin with age. She's known for years.

Her hands hang uselessly at her sides.

"Dad?" she calls softly, though it wasn't really a call anymore, only part of the ritual. She must say it for the dream to keep breathing.

No answer, of course. There never is.

The silence is thick. Too complete. She can hear her pulse inside it, slow and out of sync with everything else. The television hums beyond the door, a low static sigh she can feel in her ribs.

Heather starts forward. Each step leaves a shadowed print in the carpet. The floor creaks where it shouldn't. She tells herself she could turn back, that she's done this enough times, and that maybe the dream would let her leave now.

But the thought doesn't even make it to her hands. They lift on their own.

Her fingertips graze the wall as she passes, tracing the bumps in the paint. The light under the door flickers once. Her stomach tightens, waiting for the familiar shape that comes next. The outline of the glass on the table, the couch, the stillness.

The smell sharpens before she even touches the knob: whiskey, sweat, the faint metallic undertone that makes her teeth ache. It fills her throat, sweet and sour, and endless.

The knob is cool. It always is.

She pushes the door open.

The den exhales at her. The television's static spills across the walls, painting them silver and blue. Dust hangs in the air like tiny stars, visible only when the light stutters. A glass sits on the coffee table beside a bottle, condensation pooling beneath it. The lamp in the corner buzzes once, too bright, then dims.

"Dad?"

Her voice trembles now with a rehearsed kind of dread.

The shape on the couch is exactly where it should be: one arm limp toward the floor, the other folded against a chest that doesn't rise. The head is turned away. The shirt is wrinkled. The fabric of the couch has darkened beneath him.

Heather's breath catches. This is where it always catches.

She doesn't move closer yet. She waits for the moment when the bottle starts to fall.

And there it is.

It tips slowly, wobbling, balancing in defiance for one long second before gravity claims it. It rolls, the hollow clink barely audible under the television's hiss. It moves toward her foot with eerie precision, the same small arc it's made every single time she's dreamed this.

She crouches automatically, hands outstretched, whispering "No, no — please stop," though she knows it won't. It never does.

The bottle makes contact with her toes, rocks once, and settles.

The whiskey has spilled out this time, seeping into the carpet, spreading toward the couch leg. The scent is strong now; raw and chemical. It burns her eyes.

She looks at the spill and whispers, "I'm sorry."

The static falters. Just once. A hiccup in the signal. Then resumes, louder.

Heather rises.

Her legs feel too heavy for her body. She takes one step, then another, into the warm, stale air of the den. Each breath feels borrowed. The TV's glow flickers over her father's arm. There's a faint stain on his sleeve, something dark, rust-colored. Not fresh.

And then she hears it.

Drip.

A single note, small and wet, falling from somewhere she can't see.

Drip.

Again, closer this time. It takes her a second to realize it isn't coming from the faucet of a sink. It's hitting the carpet. A dark patch is growing wider near the couch leg, spreading into the fibers like ink.

Drip.

The sound syncs with her pulse. With each beat, it falls.

Drip.

The television flickers, bright white, and suddenly she sees it: a thin thread of red running down from his fingers, gathering at the knuckles, falling.

Her breath locks in her chest.

Drip.

Her throat tightens. She wants to stand, but her knees refuse. The carpet feels like it's gripping her, holding her in place. The air thickens with iron and static.

Drip.

She should know what happens next.

This is the part where everything pauses, and then the sound cuts, and the room holds its breath, and she whispers Dad? and the dream folds back in on itself.

It doesn't.

The drip doesn't stop.

It speeds up.

Drip drip dripdripdrip —

The separate drops smear into a continuous, wet hiss, like rain against a window that isn't there. The stain on the carpet pulses, blooming outward, then shrinking back, as if the floor itself is breathing.

The lamp in the corner buzzes too loud, until the sound frays at the edges and becomes something else.

Words.

Too low at first. Beneath hearing, beneath thought. Then

rising.

…there…

…look there….

…look….

Her scalp prickles.

She forces her gaze up, back to the couch. To the arm that hangs slack. To the hand.

The fingers are no longer still.

They twitch. Just once. A small, jerky movement, like a puppet string pulled by an unsteady hand.

"No," she whispers.

The television sputters. The static stumbles, its rhythm wrong, then surges back, twice as loud. The screen's snow thickens, the black spaces between the white dots narrowing until it's almost solid light.

Her father's head turns.

Not all at once.

In rough increments.

A click, a pause, a click.

The muscles in his neck don't seem to do any of the work. It's as if something behind him is rotating his skull, degree by degree, forcing it toward her.

Heather's stomach drops.

The light catches his face as it turns. All the merciful blur she's grown used to in this dream is gone. No smudged features. No soft smear where his mouth should be.

She sees everything.

The pallor of his skin. The slack heaviness at the corners of his lips. The stubble darkening his jaw. The thin, dried line where red meets throat, scabbed like an old cut that never quite healed.

His eyes are open.

They don't blink.

They look past her. Past the room. Past the door. Straight at nothing.

Then his gaze lowers.

To the bottle.

His mouth opens.

What leaves his throat isn't breath or words.

It's the same static, condensed, focused, as if the TV has crawled inside of him and found a new way out. The noise pours from him, rough and thick, a buzzing that feels like standing under a swarm of invisible insects.

The static swells. The sound presses in on her from all sides.

Heather flinches. She clamps her hands over her ears. Her fingers dig into her scalp, but the sound slides in between them anyway, effortless, as if her palms aren't there.

The room shudders.

The photograph on the floor rattles against its broken glass. The lamp sways once, its chain clinking. The air temperature drops so fast that her breath comes out in a faint, white cloud.

She squeezes her eyes shut.

The static drops.

Drip.

The silence that follows feels coated, as if the sound left its weight behind.

Drip.

The drop lands close enough that she feels a fleck of warmth hit her ankle.

She opens her eyes.

The stain is closer than it should be. It has crawled across the carpet toward her, following the weave of the fibers, leaving a faint reddish shadow trailing behind like a snail's path.

Her heel is wet.

She jerks her foot back. The carpet pulls with it. The threads cling to her skin like tiny hands, then snap free one by one with a soft, tearing sensation she feels in her bones.

She stares.

Her father hasn't moved. His face is still turned toward the bottle, jaw hanging slack, eyes wide and wrong.

The television is no longer showing static.

She doesn't recognize what's on the screen. The image swims, blurred, all white and gray and trembling motion. Then it snaps into focus.

It's the den.

Not as it looks now. As it should look.

As it did look.

The couch at the far wall. The lamp. The table. The exact angle of the picture frames. The pattern in the carpet where the fibers are thin.

On the floor in front of the couch, a girl sits cross-legged, her back to the screen, hair flaming red at the ends in the white-blue light.

Her shoulders rise and fall too fast.

Heather can't move. She watches herself watching.

The girl on the screen lifts a hand. Reaches for something.

The bottle.

It sits where it always sits, between her and the couch, tilted slightly, the glass catching the TV's light.

The girl's fingers wrap around it.

Heather feels the cool of glass beneath her own fingers at the same time.

She didn't mean to reach for it. She doesn't remember

reaching at all. But her hand is there, around the neck of the bottle, the curve of it fitting her grip like it was molded that way.

Her heart beats against her palm. Or maybe that's the bottle.

The liquid inside sloshes once, slow, syrupy.

There's something else inside.

She lifts it closer. Her throat works around a swallow that doesn't go anywhere.

Within the curve of the glass, clinging to its inner wall, a pale strip of paper curls. The edges are soft and fuzzed, the way paper gets after soaking too long. Ink spiderwebs across it in tight black lines that bleed into one another.

She squints. The letters squirm, too small, too far, too warped by the curve.

The TV flickers. The girl on the screen does the same thing at the same time — raises the bottle, peers in. Their movements sync, a dragged-out mirror.

Heather's stomach lurches.

"Don't," she whispers, but she doesn't know if she's talking to herself or the girl.

The room leans. Just a little. As if the floor is no longer flat but slanting, sliding everything toward the couch. Toward him.

The lamp's chain swings. The shadows on the wall stretch, thin and tall, like figures standing just out of the corner of her eye.

The door behind her clicks.

Pressure builds in her ears, like altitude rising.

Heather's fingers find the edge of the cork. She digs her nails under it. The glass is wet where the blood has reached it, slick against her skin.

She pulls.

The cork doesn't move.

She tightens her grip until her knuckles ache. Her nails bend. The cork stays where it is, a small, stubborn plug holding the paper and the liquor and the dark inside.

She braces the bottom of the bottle against the carpet and uses both hands. The neck of the bottle bites into the soft skin of her palms.

It doesn't budge.

Her reflection swims in the glass.

Only it isn't quite right.

Her eyes are wrong — too large, too dark, swallowing more white than they should. Her mouth looks too wide. The angle of her jaw is off, like someone drew her from memory and got one line crooked.

She watches herself in the bottle.

The reflected version of her opens its mouth.

Static pours out.

No sound leaves Heather's lips. She feels her throat strain as she gasps, as she sucks in air through clenched teeth, but the noise that touches her ears is the ragged hiss of white noise, torn from her mirror image's open mouth and channeled through invisible speakers.

She wants to scream, but it only comes out as feedback.

The TV crackles. The image of the girl jerks, lagging, freezing on single frames. Her hand at her mouth, her head tipped back, her eyes wide — before jumping ahead again, each version of her a fraction of a second more panicked.

The carpet under her palms pulses.

A slow, steady throb, like something is beating beneath it; buried under floorboards and insulation.

Thump.

The stain creeps farther. It has reached her shins now, soaking into the thin cotton of her pajama pants, climbing with a mind of its own.

The picture frame on the ground trembles. Glass shards jump in place. A crack splits further, a faint squeal like tiny teeth biting through.

Behind her, past the door, the world moves.

She hears it.

A sound she knows too well.

Wheels.

Small, metal, and stubborn, rolling over something hard. Their rhythm is uneven - a bump, a squeak, a clatter, as if one wheel sticks on every revolution.

They pass outside the door. Slow.

Her breath hitches. There is no hallway like that here. No surface for wheels to make those sounds.

One wheel squeals, sharp and wet, like metal crying.

Silence drops like a sheet.

And then the banging starts.

It slams through the door.

One hit, like a fist.

Another, lower, like a shoulder.

A third, heavier, as if something much larger is throwing its weight against the wood, begging entrance or demanding it.

The knob shudders in its latch.

Heather twists her head toward the sound. Her neck feels stiff, rusted, like the motion scrapes.

"Stop," she croaks. "Stop, stop."

The blows don't.

They grow more frantic. The frame rattles in the wall; the hinges creak. Plaster dust floats down in a pale drift, catching the light like snow.

She's sure it's going to splinter inward in jagged shards.

"Let me out," she whispers, though she hasn't moved toward it.

The shadows along the baseboards gain crisp edges. The lines of the door grow too defined, like they've been redrawn in darker ink. The couch's outline thickens. Her father's profile looks carved instead of slumped.

The stain on the carpet stops spreading outward and starts creeping in a straight line toward the bottle. It wraps around the bottom of it like a slow, closing hand. Crawling upward, hugging the glass.

The bottle vibrates. A faint, high whine rises from it, like air escaping through something too tight to give.

The paper inside jumps.

Ink curls and twists, forming themselves into lines that almost make sense. She inches closer, in defiance of her racing heart.

A word emerges, stark and distinct.

LEAVING

She blinks, adjusting her focus. The next phrase struggles into view; letters snapping into place.

WON'T

The air thickens. Each breath feels like dragging in fabric.

CHANGE

The final letters blur and run together. Her eyes sting; tears trace heated lines down her cheeks.

She realizes she's whispering the words.

Leaving won't change —

The banging stops.

The silence that follows is worse.

Her father's head has tilted farther. His chin hangs at an angle that would break a living neck. His eyes have rolled slightly in their sockets, enough that they seem to be looking just past her ear.

His jaw twitches.

The static tries to break free again, buzzing at the edges of his lips, but doesn't quite emerge. This time, what comes out is low and gurgling.

"Hea—"

The syllable melts into a wet choke.

She can't breathe. The room has taken all the air and packed it into the walls, the ceiling, anywhere but where she is.

The door behind her shakes suddenly, as if something on the other side has slammed both hands against it in frustration.

Don't open it.

The sentence slips into her mind like a chill draft under a door. It doesn't sound like his voice — no, it doesn't resonate with anyone she knows. It's simply there.

Her hands feel clammy. She hasn't dared to look at them since she reached for the bottle.

It tumbles away from her grip.

The glass makes a dull thud against the carpet, rolling a few inches before coming to a stop.

She plants her heels into the fibers of the carpet, attempting to push herself back, but the strands cling stubbornly between her toes. The dark stain swells with her, unwilling to let go.

She considers rising to her feet, but her knees betray her.

The couch lets out a weary creak.

Her father's arm rises, an awkward, stilted motion. The elbow bends with a hesitant delay, the wrist trailing behind, each part of him out of sync, as if they are all reluctant to follow the command.

His fingers hover, loose and unsteady, above her head.

Then, it descends.

Not to its accustomed place beside the couch.

But directed at her.

The knuckles make an unwelcome touch against her scalp, that feels more like a cold slap than a caress, as if it has long since forgotten the meaning of tenderness.

She stifles a sob, one that nearly breaks free but gets caught in her throat.

"I'm sorry," she whispers again, uselessly. "I'm sorry, I'm sorry, I'm —"

But the phrase splinters, fraying at the edges.

"I'm sorry" dissolves into static.

The bottle rolls, gliding smoothly across the carpet, a slow-motion shamble toward her knees, pulled by an invisible force that seems to hold a sinister intent all its own.

It comes to rest against her leg, the impact soft, yet the message trapped inside vibrates with urgency, like a warning being delivered with violent clarity, as if it has been struck with the weight of truth.

The paper faces her fully now. The ink has bled, but the message has shifted— or perhaps it was always this way, and her mind has deceived her.

YOU LEFT ME HERE

The letters pulse in sync with the throbbing beneath the carpet. Her throat tightens.

"No," she wheezes. "No, you left me. You left me."

Her father's lips move again, but this time there's no sound, no static. Yet she senses something, a whisper submerged in the drip.

Help

helphelphelphelphelp

It rides the descent of each silent drop, so swift and soft that she wouldn't perceive it if it didn't strike somewhere deep within her chest at the same moment. Her lungs constrict. The door shutters. A slow scrape echoes from the other side; a sound that resembles fingernails, metal, or even bone.

The knob twists, then twists again. Every noise in the room sharpens, even the drip. What remains is a thin, high-pitched whine in her ears. Her father's gaze locks onto hers.

"You always come back," he whispers, though she's unsure if it's spoken aloud or etched into her mind in the same ink as the note.

"You always come back."

The carpet pulses once more, harder this time. The room inhales. The walls lean in, the ceiling dips; the corners stretch, drawing closer as if the entire space is folding in, and collapsing around her.

On the TV screen, the girl lifts her head. She bears Heather's features.

No, not quite.

Her eyes are too dark, full of nothing but shadow — a pair of hollow wells. Her mouth stretches wider than it should, her jaw unhinges just a fraction too far.

Static erupts from her, hitting Heather in waves; it collides with her chest, her teeth, her eyes, her ears. Stinging, buzzing beneath her skin, a hundred tiny electrical burns igniting all at once.

Everything spirals inward until the room reduces to nothing but his eyes, the bottle, and that relentless line echoing in her mind: *you always come back.* It blares inside her like a fire alarm.

Her lips shape it once again.

"Dad?"

Then, the world plunges into darkness.

Chapter 13

Her whole body knew before her eyes opened.

Not the way it had in the nightmare, with no static, no dripping, no bottle trying to roll on the floor, but with a quieter alarm, a low-level hum that made her skin feel one size too small. She lay still and let it run through her, a slow scan from scalp to toes.

Nothing moved, and when the moment held, it settled back into just her room.

The radiator ticked once in its sleep, then went back to pretending it was part of the wall. Outside the window, light pressed against the thin blinds, a gray, sullen glow that didn't quite qualify as morning.

She opened her eyes.

The ceiling looked wrong. Too low, as if it had sagged in the night, leaning down to read her thoughts. Her heart thudded, waiting for space around her to tilt, or darken, to turn into the den again.

It didn't.

The blanket twisted around her legs, still damp with the sweat she hadn't fully escaped.

"You're awake," she whispered to herself. Her voice sounded like it belonged to someone who'd been crying, even though she couldn't remember if she had.

The afterimage of the dream clung anyway.

Drip.

Help.

You always come back.

Heather swallowed hard. The back of her throat tasted like metal and sleep.

It came before she could think it: the prickle between her shoulder blades, the animal sense that eyes had settled on her from somewhere just outside her field of view. She didn't move her head, only her gaze, sliding it to the side as if that would keep from spooking whatever it was.

The shelf.

Her eyes landed there first. The old plush piglet, the snow globe with the ice skater who was locked mid-spin, the worn photograph of her old life.

They were where they should be.

Except.

She pushed herself up onto her elbows, the bandage on her arm tugging, a dull burn under the gauze. The room swam once and steadied. She narrowed her eyes at the shelf.

The snow globe sat a few inches closer to the edge than it had yesterday.

She was sure of it. A faint crescent of dust traced the wood behind where the glass usually rested. Now it overlapped that line, casting a fat little circle of distortion onto the wall.

Her stomach clenched.

"I didn't move you," she told it, quietly.

It said nothing; instead, it held its breath, flakes frozen in place over the miniature figurine. But the way the glass bulged and bent the light made it look like an eye. An unblinking eye that had shuffled closer in the night to get a better look at her.

She swung her legs over the side of the bed, toes searching for the cool rectangle of the floor. Her feet found it. Solid. She stood, slowly, feeling her joints complain a little.

The desk waited, chair tucked neatly in. The blanket on the bed slumped in a familiar, defeated heap. Nothing obviously wrong or broken.

Still, that watching feeling crawled up her spine, as if the corners had grown eyes overnight.

She crossed to the shelf.

Up close, the dust ring behind the snow glow was undeniable. A thin, lighter crescent, like a halo that glass had abandoned. Her fingers hovered over it, not quite touching.

"Maybe I bumped you," she said under her breath. "Maybe I… I don't remember."

The last part came out smaller.

She tried to picture herself last night coming back from the hallway, from the phone, and from Ben's careful voice; moving around the room, reaching for the globe without noticing. It wouldn't resolve. The memory stuttered. She remembered sitting on the bed. She remembered the vent. She remembered whispering *"You're safe,"* as if it might change its meaning if she said it enough times.

She did not remember touching the snow globe.

Heather wrapped her hand around it. The glass was colder than it should have been, a chill that sank into her palm and sat there. She lifted it an inch, then set it back deliberately in the exact center of the dust ring.

A perfect fit.

"There," she muttered.

The flakes inside hadn't moved. Static snow over a static

skater. But the iced pond was darker this morning. The little painted figurine looked a fraction smaller, as if it had shrunk in the night.

You always come back.

She jerked her hand away.

"That was a dream," she said sharply. "It was just a dream."

Her gaze flicked to the door.

The feeling of being watched shifted, less like an eye and more like a presence standing just outside, ear tilted toward the wood. The thin man's posture from the hallway flickered across her mind; the way he'd leaned toward the wall like the building was telling him a secret.

Her pulse sped up.

She rubbed at her face with her free hand, fingers scraping over tired skin. "You're jumpy because you didn't sleep well," she told herself. "You're jumpy because of Donna and the case. Because of… everything."

Everything.

It was the right word and too small at the same time.

She stepped away from the shelf, needing distance from the glass, from the snow globe, and from the possibility that it had shifted on its own.

The bed looked like a place where bad dreams waited patiently for her to lie down again. The desk looked like a place she'd have to sit and think about things she didn't want to name. The whole room suddenly became a jar someone had put her in and forgotten on a shelf.

"I need air," she whispered.

The idea of staying here made her chest ache.

Her hand drifted toward the door handle.

The metal was cool and perfectly ordinary under her fingers.

No banging on the other side. No wheels. No drip. Just the faint murmur of the building's hum, leaking in around the frame.

She hesitated once, listening.

No voices. No footsteps. Just that low, electrical sigh that meant the lights and vents and old wiring were doing their quiet work behind the walls.

"Just the hallway," she told herself. "Just people."

The feeling of being watched pressed a little harder between her shoulder, like a hand urging her forward. The snow globe gleamed on the shelf behind her, perfectly centered now, perfectly innocent.

She didn't look at it again.

Heather turned the knob and stepped out.

The hallway met her with a wash of cooler air and the low, steady hum of the building. Fluorescent lights buzzed overhead, soft but insistent, giving everything that faintly washed-out look she'd started to think of as this place's default expression.

Heather let the door ease shut behind her until the latch caught. The sound was small, neat, and contained.

The floor out here was a different texture than the one in her dream; smooth, polished, too clean. She stared at it anyway, waiting for dark stains to appear beneath her bare toes, some slow creep of red she'd missed.

Nothing.

"See?" she muttered. "Normal."

Her voice sounded too loud in the empty stretch of hallway. The air tasted vaguely of coffee and cleaner; somewhere, distant, a vacuum whined and cut off. Doors lined both sides of the hall, most of them closed. One down the way was propped half-open with a shoe, faint music leaking out.

She walked.

Her bandaged arm ached in time with each step. The sleeve of her shirt stuck there a little, reminding her of the rusted screw, the coffee stain, and the way the stairwell had leaned around her.

Halfway to the corner, she slowed.

She could see the phone alcove from here with the small table where the handset rested, the black cord coiled beneath it like a sleeping snake. Above it, the same cheap clock as always ticked out a rhythm that never matched her heartbeat.

She looked at the phone, then away.

Ben's voice from last night brushed across her mind, careful and measured. You are safe. We'll talk when I get back. Let the people around you carry some of this.

She'd hung up on him, in the end.

Her stomach knotted tightly. Determined, she pushed herself forward, glancing past the phone, the ticking clock, and the bulletin board cluttered with fliers and notices: yoga class, maintenance work, a handwritten note about lost keys.

A door slammed somewhere down the hall, the sound crashing into her with unexpected force. Heather flinched as it ricocheted in a strange, uneven manner, making the hallway feel longer than it truly was. She thought she caught a faint sound behind the door, but it vanished too quickly to comprehend.

She paused, straining to listen.

Her eyes followed the direction of the noise. The door remained shut.

Just then, someone nearly bumped into her around the corner.

"Whoa, sorry!"

It was the woman from the courtyard who halted abruptly, nearly losing her balance while holding a pile of neatly folded towels against her chest. A loose strand of hair escaped her bun, which stuck to her cheek, as she brushed it away with her elbow. "Didn't see you there."

"It's okay," Heather said automatically, even though her heart had just lurched hard enough to make her see white.

Up close, the woman's eyes were the same kind as in the courtyard: warm, tired, entirely too observant.

Her wristband flashed when she shifted her grip.

"Rough night?" the woman asked lightly.

They landed like a hand to the chest.

Heather's mouth went dry. "What?"

The woman nodded toward Heather's face, then her bandaged arm. "You look like you fought the pillow and lost. Also, you're a little pale. Do you, uh…" her voice dipped, "want one of these?" She tilted the top towel. "They're actually clean. I swear."

Heather forced a breath out, "No. Thank you. I'm fine."

There it was again. The word everyone seemed to be stacking on top of her lately, like a paperweight.

"You sure?" the woman pressed. "I heard… something last night. Or I thought I did. Maybe a bad dream?" She shrugged, like she was offering an out, not digging. "Walls are thin. Sorry if you heard me, too. I swear my brain sets its alarm to three a.m. now for no reason."

A dream.

Heather's mind zipped back to the den, to the bottle, to the pounding on the door.

"No," she said too fast. "I — I'm okay. Just didn't sleep much."

The woman studied her for half a beat longer, then let it go. "Well. If you feel like escaping your four walls again, the courtyard's decent this morning. Less wind. More birds. Same terrible coffee stand."

Heather nodded without promising anything.

The woman adjusted the towels. "See you around, neighbor."

She headed past, toward the open door with the muss. As she went, Heather heard her call over her shoulder, "Don't let the walls win, okay?"

Don't let the walls win.

What did that even mean?

Heather stood there, watching her until she vanished around the bend. The hallway seemed to push gently against her from all sides.

Her gaze slipped, almost against her will, to the far end of the corridor.

Empty.

No tall figure or hood to be seen.

She should have been relieved.

Instead, the emptiness was worse, like the space where he ought to be had become its own kind of presence.

"Just people," she whispered. "Just doors. Just… here."

Her feet moved again before her brain decided where they were going. Past another door, this one with a faint scuff mark near the bottom where something had been kicked against it too often. Past a framed print of a landscape so generic it barely registered as a place at all.

She almost made it to the corner before someone else stepped into her path.

This time, it was a man in a faded polo with a ring of keys at his hip. He gave her a polite, worn-out smile, the kind people used when they weren't sure if conversation was welcome.

"Morning," he said. "Everything alright?"

She wanted to answer honestly, *There's blood in my dreams, and bottles whisper, and someone was listening through the walls, and I don't know what's real anymore.*

"Fine," she said.

His eyes flicked toward the bandage on her arm. "Hope that's not from those stairs. They trip people up."

Heather instinctively pulled the arm closer to her body. "Just a slip."

"Gotcha." He nodded once.

"Well, if something's acting weird," he cleared his throat, "heat, lights, whatever, just flag me down."

He moved on without waiting for more.

Heather watched him walk away, pulse thudding unevenly. His keys jingled softly with each step, but even after he rounded the corner, she could still hear them.

Something *was* acting weird in her place.

Everything was.

Her dream still clung to her skin, thick and cold. The image of her father's eyes following her, the bottle rolling toward her, the stain crawling across the carpet; none of it stayed behind.

She took a breath and held it a second too long.

She suddenly couldn't remember why she'd come out here at all.

Out here, she was visible. Her room, even rearranged and wrong-feeling, was at least a wrongness she recognized. Out here belonged to someone else, and she didn't trust any of them to see her right now. She turned back before her feet committed her to going farther.

She shut the door quietly this time and leaned against it,

waiting for her pulse to settle. Her gaze drifted over the room automatically, tracing the same landmarks she had previously.

And then she stilled.

The blanket on her bed was smooth.

Not just straightened, but stretched flat, corners aligned, a crease running down the center as if someone had pulled the fabric tight with both hands.

She hadn't done that. She hadn't even touched it except for when she slept.

Something inside her folded in on itself. The instinct to double-check the rest of the room flared, but she forced herself to breathe through it, slow and even. *People make beds.* That was a reasonable thought. A harmless thought. But it didn't feel harmless. It was an accusation pressed neatly into cotton.

She moved toward the bed anyway, compelled by something between dread and disbelief. The blanket didn't show a single impression, not one wrinkle from where she had sat earlier. It looked like someone else's bed entirely. Hers had never looked this tidy.

"I didn't do this," she whispered, fingers hovering an inch above the fabric. She didn't touch it. Couldn't.

Something shifted near the door, a soft scrape, paper against the floor. Heather spun.

A small rectangle poked out from beneath the door, just enough for her to see the edge of it. Her breath hitched. She took a hesitant step, then another. The paper didn't move.

It hadn't been there when she came in.

Her fingertips trembled as she crouched to reach for it. She slid it out, expecting some kind of advertisement, a menu, or a flyer.

But the front of the paper was blank except for a single word scrawled in shaky black ink:

LOOK.

Her knees wobbled. The hallway beyond the door was suddenly too quiet, as if whatever had left it were still there, waiting.

Her thumb smudged a corner of the page.

"Look where?" she whispered.

Heather held the paper between her fingers as if it might burn her. The word kept vibrating in her skull: LOOK.

Not a suggestion.

More of a command. A warning. A clue.

She stood in the middle of her room, trying to breathe evenly, but her chest kept tightening in small, unpredictable squeezes. She turned the paper over. The back was blank. No room number. No logo. No cute newsletter clipart. No handwriting she recognized.

Someone wanted her attention.

But on what?

Her gaze dragged across the room, moving from object to object. The snow globe. The shelf. The blanket. The narrow strip of light on the floor. None of them looked wrong, but the wrongness was everywhere anyway.

Fear reshapes things. Ben had said as much. Donna had implied it, too. *Patterns.* People who break don't break at once. They crack.

"Okay," she murmured to herself, backing away. "Fine. I'm looking."

Her heart raced. She examined the shelf.

Then peered beneath it.

Checked the desk drawers.

Glanced toward the bathroom, pushing the door ajar just

enough to glimpse the sink, the mirror, and the silence suspended in between.

Everything was in order.

She checked behind the curtain.

Then peeked under the bed.

Each emptiness only amplified the thudding of her heart, until her ribs might tremble apart.

She checked the door once more. Nothing. No shadow lurking by the gap, no hidden notes, no footsteps fading away. Whoever had slipped it through had vanished.

Or perhaps they were still watching her.

The thought flashed through her mind before she could suppress it. A chill ran down her spine. She turned slowly to face the small mirror perched above her desk.

Her reflection waited there, pale and stretched at the edges, but undeniably hers. She leaned in, searching for signs of distortion or a flicker of something amiss.

Nothing.

Just her.

But LOOK.

Look where? Look at what?

Pressing the heel of her hand to her forehead, she murmured, "Think. Think. Think."

She understood the word. That wasn't the problem. The problem was how many meanings crowded behind it at once.

She crossed to her desk, spotting the small white envelope Ben had pressed into her hand two days prior. *"Just in case,"* he'd said, and it lay tucked underneath her notebook, its corner just peeking out like a secret that begged to remain hidden.

She touched it with one fingertip, and a wave of nausea stirred in her stomach.

If you get overwhelmed, take one.

If things feel distorted, take one.

If the fear starts writing its own narrative again... take one.

Heather shoved the envelope further beneath the papers until it vanished from view.

She wasn't lost or overwhelmed. She wouldn't take something that clouded her judgment and made her easier to overlook.

Not now.

Not with everything coming into focus around her.

Her heart stuttered.

She realized she hadn't checked the window.

Crossing the room, her hands shook more now. The window was cool and mundane. She wiped the morning dew off the glass, then noticed something shift below.

Heather recoiled so quickly that she collided with the desk.

A bend of shadow retreating beyond the edge of her window. Too tall and thin.

Her breath escaped in a jagged rush.

"No. No, no no —"

She pressed her palms towards the air and stepped back.

LOOK.

She had looked.

And something had looked back.

The paper slipped from her grasp, fluttering to the floor, landing face-up. LOOK seemed to glare at her, unyielding.

She sank onto the edge of the bed, careful to disturb the blanket as little as possible, wrapping her arms around herself.

Chapter 14

Trapped in the posture she'd curled herself into, Heather sat on the edge of the bed, arms wrapped tight around her ribs as if holding herself together by pressure alone. She hadn't moved since the shadow slipped away beneath her window, not really. Maybe her fingers had twitched. Maybe she'd blinked, but her body was still molded into the shape of fear, braced like something was about to strike again.

The room held its breath with her.

The note lay where she'd dropped it, the single word staring up at her from the floor, LOOK, as if waiting for her to follow instructions she never wanted.

She couldn't remember how long she'd been sitting here. A minute, or ten, or the full distance between this morning and now. Her sense of time had frayed; the edges curled up like burnt paper. The light through the blinds hadn't changed much. It was still gray and thin.

Her breath was shallow and uneven.

In.

Shiver.

Out.

Hold.

Repeat.

She tried to relax her shoulders, but they refused. Every muscle along her neck was wired directly into the part of her mind that kept scanning the corners for movement.

Nothing moved.

But the wrongness from earlier hadn't left. It had just settled, like dust after a collapse, waiting for her to disturb it again.

She forced her gaze up from the floor.

The room was her room; her shelf, her knick-knacks, the window, the desk, the too-neat blanket, but it didn't look familiar. Not the way it usually did. It was as if everything had been placed back just slightly off.

Heather swallowed hard.

Routine.

Routine was supposed to anchor her.

Ben said structure steadied the mind.

She straightened a fraction and tried to reach for that idea. She could get up, splash water on her face, and make the bed, but it was already made. That thought landed like a bruise.

Her heartbeat flickered.

She pressed her palms to her knees, grounding herself in the pressure of her own hands.

"You're okay," she whispered, voice rough at the edges. "You're just… shaken. Anyone would be."

But the lie didn't even try to sound convincing. Her body wasn't responding like she was shaken. It was responding like she'd been dropped into the wrong skin and was trying, frantically, to climb back into the right one.

She let out a breath that trembled all the way to her fingertips.

The walls hummed faintly. She'd always told herself it was the old wiring, the vents, the building doing whatever buildings did behind their surfaces.

Slow breath.

Measured breath.

Not hers.

Her spine tightened.

Don't listen.

Don't lean toward it.

Don't let the walls win.

Heather lifted her hands to her temples and pressed, as if she could keep her thoughts from splitting further outward, fracturing into every dark possibility.

"You need to move," she whispered. "You need to do something normal."

Normal.

She didn't know what counted as normal anymore; sitting still didn't feel normal, but standing didn't feel normal either.

Still, she forced her body upward, slowly, like a puppet testing its strings. Her legs trembled as she stared at the note again.

"Not now."

She stepped over it and toward the window. She didn't want to look out again, but pretending she wasn't thinking about it was worse.

No movement below. Her reflection ghosted in the glass, pale and stretched, but not wrong enough to terrify her. "Routine," she murmured. "Just... start."

She crossed toward the desk and flattened her hand on the wood, grounding herself in the texture and solidity. Her fingers brushed the papers, the hidden envelope beneath them, and the corner of the notebook she'd abandoned.

Her breath hitched. Her body wasn't calming, and routine wasn't helping. If anything, the normal actions made the wrongness louder.

Heather closed her eyes.

Her voice came out small but steady, "I don't want to be alone."

But she was. More now than she'd been in days.

She reached for her notebook, the same one where she used to write her secrets. Her fingers brushed the cover, but the pages were foreign now, as if they belonged to a version of her who still believed naming things could keep them contained.

She flipped it open anyway.

Blank page.

A single line at the top, crooked from where the pen had snagged the paper:

Don't let the walls win.

She stared at it, pulse fluttering. She hadn't written that. She would remember writing that. The ink was dark, still a little glossy in the right angle of light.

Her throat tightened as she tore the page out.

The rip was too loud, the sound bouncing oddly around the room, as if the walls were tossing it between them. She balled the paper in her fist, but her hand wouldn't clench enough to drop it. It sat there in her palm, dampening with sweat.

Walls lingered, pulled from somewhere earlier, though she couldn't quite place where.

"Don't let the walls win."

But what if that wasn't advice?

What if that was a warning?

She pried her fingers open and set it back on the desk without smoothing it out. Her movements were deliberate, exaggerated as she went to the sink and turned on the tap, watching the water rush out clear and unremarkable. She cupped it in her hands and splashed her face once, then again. Cold steadied her more than warmth ever had.

"Okay."

Her voice sounded thin.

She dried her hands on the hem of her shirt and leaned against the counter, breathing through her nose, counting without counting. The hum in the walls continued, constant and low.

Good. Or bad. She couldn't tell anymore.

Heather turned back and let her gaze land where it wanted instead of where she told it to. The desk. The bed. The door. The shelf. Nothing lunged forward. Nothing whispered.

She crossed to the desk once again and reached beneath the stack of papers to pull out the small white envelope Ben had given her. It was light in her hand.

Just in case, he'd said.

If things spike.

If you need help taking the edge off.

She turned it over once, then again. No label. No instructions in his handwriting. Just a folded flap, sealed and patient. The idea that swallowing something could make all of this quieter was like a lie designed for someone else — someone less alert, less terrified of what she might lose if her thoughts dulled.

She slid the envelope into the drawer and shut it, harder than necessary.

"No," she said aloud. "Not like that."

Saying it helped a little.

Sitting still made the room feel like it was closing in, but pacing was too much like running. She compromised by moving with purpose; straightening the chair, aligning the notebook with the desk's edge, and adjusting the scrambled papers by an inch. Small corrections. Proof of agency.

When she reached the door, her hand hovered over the handle.

She didn't want to go back into the hallway. She didn't want to see anyone who might ask how she was doing in that careful voice that meant *answer* correctly. But staying here was worse. Like agreeing to something without knowing what it was.

Heather rested her forehead briefly against the cool wood of the door and closed her eyes.

"I just need to remind myself," she whispered. "That I can leave if I want to."

The sentence lingered longer than it should have.

Turning the handle, she stepped into the hallway. This time, she didn't hesitate. The hallway looked the same as always — long, bright, deceptively normal.

She took a few steps before halting. The feeling didn't spike this time. It stayed, low and steady.

Heather gulped, forcing herself to move forward.

She was uncertain of where she was going, but all she knew was that standing still was no longer an option. Deep within her, past the clamor of anxiety, something firmer began to take hold.

* * *

Ben's office had always been the place where things slowed down. Where voices lowered, where questions waited their turn, and the world stopped rushing her long enough for her to catch up.

The walk there stretched longer than usual.

She stopped outside the door and stared at the nameplate.

It was still there. Same font. Same muted brass. Same careful alignment.

Relief loosened something in her chest.

She reached for the handle.

It turned easily at first, just enough to make her believe she was welcome, then stopped short with a soft resistance that had nothing to do with a lock and everything to do with permission.

A small red light glowed near the frame.

She frowned and tried again, slower this time, as if gentleness might persuade it.

The door opened no farther than just a few inches, halted by something unseen. Heather stared at the gap, at the sliver of dim light beyond it.

"I just need a minute," she murmured to the door.

Heather swallowed, eyes scanning, cataloging.

The office looked the same at first glance: the couch against the wall, the low table, the lamp with the shade that always sat slightly crooked. But the air smelled different. Less eucalyptus and more cleaner, like someone had wiped the room down until it complied.

Her skin tightened.

On the desk: a stack of files she didn't recognize. Not the messy, lived-in piles Ben always pretended he had under control. These were squared, aligned, and edges flush as someone had measured them. A pen lay parallel to the desk blotter. The computer monitor was dark.

On the low table beside the couch: no glass of water.

That should not have mattered. It was nothing. A detail small enough to disappear the moment she noticed it.

But the last time she'd sat here, there had been a glass. Half-full. Condensation gathering at the base, slowly spreading into a ring on the coaster as he talked.

Now the coaster was bare.

Heather pressed her hand to the door frame as if she could steady herself against it.

Her gaze slid to the corner of the desk where the picture frame had been.

The space was empty.

Heather stared until her eyes burned.

She could still see the photo in her mind: them caught mid-movement, edges softened by the light above, his arm around her in a way that was easy instead of posed.

He had laughed right after it was taken.

Not at the picture, but at her — the way she'd tried to pull away the second she realized someone was watching, like being seen mattered more than being held. He hadn't let go right away. Just tightened his arm for half a second, enough to keep her there, and make it feel like staying was a choice instead of something she'd been guided into.

"Relax," he'd said, softer than usual, close enough that she'd felt it more than heard it. "You're allowed to exist in a moment without bracing for it to end."

She hadn't known what to do with that.

A laugh rose in her throat and fell flat. How quickly the world could remove something and pretend it had never been there at all.

"Maybe I imagined it," she thought, and the thought landed like a slap.

She backed away from the door, palms damp.

She could leave. She should leave. This wasn't hers. This was his — his space, his work, his boundaries. Normal people didn't try door handles and inventory desks in places like this.

But normal had left her days ago and hadn't bothered to say goodbye.

Heather leaned in again, closer to the gap, voice dropping to a whisper as if the room might hear it.

"Why would you take it down?"

No answer.

She shifted her weight, and the door creaked softly. The light on the frame now blinked and projected a small continuous beep.

Heather froze.

From deeper down the hall came footsteps. Not rushing, but steady.

She straightened, stepping back from the door as if she'd been caught with her hand in a jar.

"Can I help you?"

A woman stood a few feet down the hall, tablet tucked against her side, expression polite but guarded.

"He told me he'd be gone," Heather said, too quickly. "Conference. I just —" she swallowed. "I need something."

The woman nodded as if that made sense.

Heather glanced again at the red light.

She adjusted the tablet under her arm. "Is everything okay?"

There it was again. The question that pretended to be gentle was a trap, dressed up as concern. *Are you okay? Really okay? Everything okay?* The same shape every time, as people had agreed on a script.

"I'm fine."

The woman's eyes flicked to Heather's bandaged arm. The edge of the gauze peeked under her sleeve like a confession. Her expression softened by a fraction.

"Do you need someone to call?"

Heather's pulse jumped. *Call* lit up every nerve in her body. Call who? Holly? Who had said she couldn't do this again. Ben? Who wasn't here, and question her on why she was trying to break into his office.

"No," Heather said sharply. Then quieter, "No. I just… I left something in there."

The woman looked at the cracked door again. "If it's important, I can get it for you. If you tell me what it is."

Heather stared at her. The offer was reasonable. That was the problem. Reasonable didn't feel safe anymore. Reasonable felt like a hand on the back of her neck, steering her toward a version of the story she didn't control.

"It's not… an object," Heather murmured, and heard how strange that sounded. "It's… forget it."

The woman held her gaze, then nodded carefully. "Okay."

She didn't move away or step in. She just stayed, a quiet presence in the hall that made Heather feel visible in all the wrong ways.

Heather's eyes drifted back to the empty corner of the desk. She couldn't stop them. The absence pulled her like gravity.

The woman followed her gaze through the gap. "Was there something on his desk you needed?" she asked.

Heather's throat tightened. *She should lie and say a notebook or a folder.* Something normal, but the truth came out anyway.

"There was a picture."

The woman blinked. "A picture."

Heather nodded. "In a frame. Right there." She lifted her hand and pointed at the empty space, as if it could testify for her. "It was… important."

The woman's expression didn't change much, but something

in her eyes shifted; recognition, maybe, or caution. "He takes things with him sometimes," she said gently. "If it was personal, he might've packed it."

Packed it.

The phrase made Heather's stomach turn.

She imagined the frame slid into a suitcase between folded shirts. Imagine him pulling it out in some hotel room and setting it on a dresser next to a lamp, like a tiny altar. Imagine him doing that with someone else watching, with someone else laughing in the background of the call.

"No," Heather whispered, before she meant to.

The woman's brows drew together. "No?"

Heather's hand dropped as her fingers curled tight against her palm. "It was here," she huffed. "I saw it."

The woman's face softened further.

"Hey," she said. "Okay. I hear you."

It sent heat through Heather's chest. *I hear you.* Not, *I believe you.* Not, *you're right.* Just, I hear you, like she was a sound, and not a person.

Heather took a step back, away from the door and the woman.

"I shouldn't be here. I'm sorry."

"You don't have to apologize," the woman replied immediately. "It's okay. It's just — he's not available right now."

Not available.

Heather nodded, once, mechanically. She turned as if her body had decided before her mind caught up.

As she walked away, she could feel the office staring at her back like an eye. The light glinted in the corner of her vision. The space on the desk stayed empty, swallowing all her arguments whole.

Behind her, the woman hesitated, then called gently, "If you need anything, there are other people here. You don't have to handle it alone."

Heather kept walking.

Other people. The phrase was a hallway full of closed doors. It was the sound of someone offering help without offering herself. It was Ben's voice saying, *You're safe,* when safe was a room you weren't allowed to leave.

She reached the corner and paused, palm braced against the wall. The surface was smooth, cool, unbothered by her.

The picture frame was gone.

The glass of water was gone.

The room had been cleaned of her, without anyone asking her permission.

Heather swallowed hard, and the swallow scraped.

In her head, it returned.

LOOK.

She had, and all she could see was absence arranged neatly into place.

Chapter 15

etween one breath and the next, a voice slid through the night.

You think you're alone, but you're not.

Heather's eyes opened.

The door stood slightly open, just enough for a thin strip of light to spill across the floor. Heather's heavy eyes followed it lazily from the edge of the desk, across the floor, until the light wasn't clean anymore.

A shadow.

Her eyes lifted.

Someone stood in her doorway.

Her heart struck once, hard enough to hurt, then slowed with eerie precision.

The figure did not step forward.

It simply stood there.

Watching.

The line of their head was slightly tilted, as if considering her. The darkness clung to it differently than it clung to the rest of the room, denser, deliberate.

The memory of the thin man in the hallway, ear to the wall, flashed before her eyes; then another. Photographs, timelines, and patterns that Donna had wanted cataloged. The Autumn

Murders. Men who watched before they acted.

You think you're alone.

The voice hadn't repeated itself, but the words still vibrated in her skull.

Heather's fingers tightened slowly in the blanket.

This is it, she thought.

The figure remained still long enough for her fear to morph into anger at the realization that she was being observed. Studied. Weighed.

Her muscles began to coil.

She shifted just enough to bring her shoulders forward and to lift her head off the pillow.

The figure didn't move toward her. Instead, it shifted back, slow and deliberate, as if reconsidering its place in the room. The strip of light beneath the door widened as it retreated.

That movement snapped something in her.

It was leaving.

It had come into her space, stood over her while she slept, whispered into her mind, and now it was walking away like she was something it had finished inspecting.

Heather was on her feet before she consciously chose to be. The blanket fell away in a soft rush of fabric. Her bare feet hit the floor without hesitation, and the cold didn't register.

Without a second thought, her hand reached toward the shelf as she crossed the room. The snow globe was cool and firm in her grip, its weight a comfort from a time before fear had familiarized itself with her.

The tiny skater inside remained frozen mid-spin, oblivious of the threat.

Heather did not look at it as she moved. She stepped into the hallway.

The fluorescent lights buzzed overhead, washing everything in thin, colorless light. The floor ran long and pale toward the corner, and at the far end, something moved.

A shape detached itself from the wall; tall, narrow, with its head angled slightly, as if it had been listening. The overhead light caught only the edge of a shoulder, the line of a jaw swallowed in shadow. No face or detail to be seen.

It appeared not to notice her, as it turned slowly and stepped back toward the blind turn at the end of the hall.

Something in Heather's chest narrowed to a single, burning point. The walls fell away, the hum of the lights vanished, even her own breathing thinned until all she could see was the space between them, and the distance between them stretching with every step it took.

No more thinking.

No more wondering if she imagined that.

It was leaving.

And she would not let it.

* * *

"Stop!"

As the figure rounded the corner, Heather didn't slow; she launched. No space remained for thought or doubt. Her shoulder drove forward and struck solid resistance. The collision knocked the air from both of them in one violent exhale. They crashed to the floor together, bone against tile, skin against fabric, as the sound of impact ricocheted down the hall.

For a split second, they were tangled, disoriented — too solid to be imagined.

Then instinct took over.

Heather scrambled upward, climbing over him as he twisted beneath her. Her knees slammed into something hard: rib, hips, she didn't care, and she locked her weight down before he could roll. Her hands fisted in his collar, dragging him back when he tried to pull away.

"I know who you are!" she screamed, though she didn't really. But she knew what he was.

The thing that watched.

The thing that waited.

He bucked under her, breath hot and panicked, hands shoving at her shoulders. She barely felt it. The snow globe was already in her grip.

She lifted it high and brought it down with everything she had.

The first blow landed above his temple with a thick, cracking thud that jolted up her arm and into her teeth.

He shouted a ragged, human sound, and she swung again before the noise finished leaving his mouth.

The second strike exploded.

Glass burst outward in a spray of glitter and splintered shards. Tiny silver flakes scattered like sparks across the tile, into his hair, across her hands. Something warm struck her wrist. The globe split in her grip, jagged and vicious.

He cursed, twisting harder now, trying to roll them, but she followed the motion, clinging. She drove the broken edge down again. Each impact landed harder than the last.

Down.

Down.

Down.

Years of grief.

Years of being doubted.

Years of being misunderstood.

Years of feeling unsafe.

Her arm rose and fell as if it belonged to someone else.

He caught her forearms at last — strong hands clamping down, fingers digging hard enough to bruise. "Get off me!" he shouted, and it cut through the chaos just enough to register.

Human.

For a second, that mattered.

Then it didn't.

She tore one arm free and drove her fist into his face instead. Once. Twice. The world had narrowed to contact and resistance. Tile under her knees. His breath was hot and uneven. The metallic scent bloomed between them.

"You don't get to watch me," she spat over the pounding in her ears.

He heaved upward, nearly dislodging her, and her hand slipped on something slick. She adjusted, straddling him harder, pressing her weight down until his shoulders struck tile again.

He was not a shadow anymore.

He was solid.

And she could hurt him.

The realization fed something electric inside her.

He had come into her space.

He had stood over her while she slept.

He had whispered into her mind.

And now he was under her.

For the first time in days, she was not the one scrambling.

He tried again to shove her off, his grip slipping in the glitter and blood. His head turned, exposing the side of his face to the harsh hallway light. His mouth opened, not in a shout this time.

"Heather —"

Her name.

Not angry, or panicked.

Just familiar.

That sound struck something old in her chest.

Familiar.

Almost.

She hesitated.

Just long enough for him to suck in a breath.

That was his mistake.

She slammed her forehead forward with a brutal crack, as bone met bone. Pain flared white behind her eyes, but she barely registered it. Warmth burst between them; he shouted, and this time she heard it.

Her name. Almost clear.

But the hallway was roaring now, the fluorescent lights buzzing louder, until everything narrowed to the space between her hands and his face. She brought the broken rim of the snow globe down again as she aimed to end it.

He twisted hard beneath her as arms grabbed her from behind; first around her shoulders, then fingers locking around her wrists. She snarled and thrashed, kicking backward blindly. Someone cursed, and another shouted her name again, closer this time, almost pleading.

"You're safe — Heather, you're safe…"

It detonated inside her, as she screamed a sound that tore her throat raw and caused her to lunge forward again, despite the weight dragging her back.

Pressure bloomed suddenly on her upper arm as hands held

her tighter.

The world tilted.

The lights fractured into streaks. Voices stretched thin and rubbery, overlapping in meaningless syllables. The floor lurched too far away, then too close. Her limbs grew heavy as the strength drained from them mid-strike.

She tried to swing again.

Her arm would not lift.

The broken glass slipped from her fingers and struck the tile with a small, distant sound; her body followed an instant later.

As she went down, her vision tunneled inward, shrinking to a tight circle of light.

In that narrowing frame, she saw his face clearly for the first time.

Chapter 16

Illusion was softer than darkness.

Darkness came all at once, between a slammed door and a swallowed scream. Illusion returned in pieces.

First, the light, flat, and unblinking pressed down through her eyelids until she had no choice but to open them.

The ceiling loomed overhead, a pristine expanse of white. No trace of water damage to mar its surface, no fissure to hint at the passage of time. And yet, the absence of familiar seams between wall and corner was unnervingly alien.

Her tongue felt thick.

She tried to swallow and found the back of her throat dry and scraped raw, as if she had been screaming for a very long time.

She couldn't remember if she had.

The second thing was the weight.

Her arms would not lift.

At first, she thought she was simply too tired, that the exhaustion had finally claimed her muscles and left her pinned to the mattress by nothing more than her own body. She tried again, slower.

Her wrists did not move.

A cool band encircled each one.

Heather inhaled carefully.

The familiar scent of detergent and eucalyptus was gone, and in its place lingered something sharper, too refined, as though the air had been meticulously filtered and stripped of its essence.

The hum was here, too.

It threaded through the room the way it had threaded through the walls of her studio apartment, through the hallway lights, through the vent above her bed.

Only here, it was closer. Less like background noise and more like a presence with machinery behind it.

Her pulse began to climb.

She shifted her legs.

Another band, across her thighs and ankles.

The realization did not arrive in a scream, but in a slow tightening under her ribs.

"I—"

Her voice came out smaller than she intended, barely above the hum.

She tried again.

"Please."

The word surprised her.

She hadn't meant to say that.

Her gaze slid sideways.

Against the stark wall stood a counter, an unyielding sentinel of the room. Adjacent to it, a cart bore neatly folded cloths, their crisp lines almost taunting in their precision. On a tray, an array of small instruments lay with careful precision.

The hum deepened slightly, then settled again.

Footsteps approached.

A figure entered her field of vision from the left, moving into the overhead light without casting a long shadow. His outline was familiar in shape, but the details did not immediately attach themselves to meaning.

He stood near her shoulder.

Close enough that she could see the faint lines at the corners of his eyes.

"You're awake," he said.

His voice was calm.

Heather's heart stuttered once and then began to pound harder.

She searched his face automatically, not for confirmation of where she was or for an explanation.

For him.

For something she recognized.

The tilt of a mouth. The warmth behind the eyes. The private softness that used to exist when no one else was watching.

She found composure instead.

"What—" she tried.

Her tongue felt slow and heavy.

"What happened?"

He did not answer immediately. His gaze flicked once to the monitor behind her, then back to her face.

"You had an episode," he said.

She tried to lift her head, but the angle of the pillow held her where she was.

"I shouldn't be restrained," her voice steadier than before. "I didn't do anything."

Powell did not flinch at the accusation.

"You attacked someone," he replied calmly.

It landed without weight.

Images tried to rise.

The hallway.

The corner.

Impact.

Glass breaking.

A voice.

Safe.

Her stomach lurched.

"I defended myself," she corrected.

Her jaw tightened. "You weren't there."

His gaze didn't harden.

"Tell me what you saw."

The question almost disarmed her.

She swallowed.

"The door was open," she began. "Just a little. There was light behind him. He didn't move at first." Her pulse quickened as she spoke, the memory sharpening. "He tilted his head, like he was studying me."

Powell listened without interrupting.

"He stepped back when I sat up," she continued. "Like he didn't want me to know he'd been there. That's what made it real. That's what made it—" she stopped.

"Made it what?" he prompted.

"Intentional."

The hum behind the walls dipped lower, then steadied again. She hadn't noticed it until now, but it seemed to shift when the room quieted.

Powell nodded once, as if logging it.

"And when you followed him?"

"I wasn't following," she snapped. "I was stopping him."

"Stopping him from what?"

Her throat worked.

"From coming back."

Silence lingered between them.

He stepped toward the monitor behind her shoulder, checking something she couldn't see. When he returned to her side, he rested his hands lightly against the metal rail of the gurney.

"I saw him," she said, and heard the strain in it. "He was in my room."

Her eyes locked on his, willing him to react the way she expected.

To frown.

To say that someone would check.

Instead, he leaned slightly closer, his voice lowering into something steadier.

"You've been reporting heightened vigilance for weeks," he said carefully. "Increased startle response. Interpreting neutral stimuli as threat."

The hum continued.

"You felt threatened," he added, gently. "That doesn't mean there was a threat."

Heather's throat tightened.

That phrasing; that careful separation.

Felt.

Was.

Her fingers strained against the restraints without her permission.

"They were watching me," she whispered.

His expression did not change.

"You've been under significant stress," he said.

The words were measured and thoughtful.

And unbearably distant.

She searched his face again.

This time harder.

He glanced toward the far side of the room, toward equipment she hadn't fully looked at yet. A compact machine with tubing coiled neatly beside it.

He did not comment on it.

Instead, he returned his focus to her.

"You are here," he said. "And you are overwhelmed."

Overwhelmed.

It wasn't big enough for what lived inside her.

"I was handling it," she insisted. "I was doing what you told me to do."

His gaze sharpened slightly at that.

"What do you think I told you to do?"

She blinked.

"To ground myself. To breathe. To not let the walls win."

The phrase hung between them.

Powell's expression didn't change, but something recalibrated behind his eyes.

"And did that help?" he asked.

"For a while."

"And tonight?"

She hesitated, "no."

The admission caught hard in her throat.

"You escalated," he said quietly. "You've escalated before under stress."

Her stomach dropped.

"Before?" she echoed.

His pause was small.

"You've had similar episodes."

"When?"

The question came too fast.

Powell's hand shifted on the rail. "You don't remember?"

Cool slid down her spine, "Remember what?"

The hum shifted again, almost imperceptibly.

He chose his words with care.

"There have been periods," he said," where fear overrides interpretation. Where your brain fills gaps with threat."

"That's not an answer."

"It's the safest way to describe it."

Safe.

The word struck harder this time.

Her fingers flexed uselessly against the restraint.

"Stop saying that."

"Safe?"

She searched for language and found none that fit cleanly.

"It doesn't feel like what you mean."

She turned her head slightly, straining to see more of the room. The equipment at the periphery sharpened into clearer shape; wires, pads, a screen that glowed faintly but displayed nothing active.

Her pulse spiked.

"What is that?"

Powell followed her gaze but did not move toward it.

"It's not active," he said.

"That's not what I asked."

"It's here in case it's needed."

Needed.

The word hollowed her out.

The hum rose a fraction louder. She realized then, with a cruel clarity, that the sound was not coming from the walls alone.

"You're going to do something," she whispered.

"We're going to help you stabilize," he replied.

Her chest tightened, "Please don't."

They left her before she could stop them.

Powell paused only a fraction of a second, as something flickered across his face, then it was gone. He straightened, shoulders aligning, expression settling into something practiced.

"Okay," someone said quietly near her shoulder.

Cool fingers slipped through her hair, parting it with a deliberate slowness that sent a shiver down her spine. A damp chill nestled against her temples, creeping in like an unwelcome thought. The sharp scent of antiseptic wrapped around her, unmistakable now — a gel meticulously applied, its coldness a warning. The pads pressed against her skin, a firm grip that was both precise and disconcerting, as if they sought to hold more than just her physical form.

She tried to turn her head, but the strap across her forehead held her centered.

"Hold still," the nurse murmured.

Metal clicked softly near her ear; the low hum that had been background noise all day shifted in tone.

Her wrists strained against the restraints.

"Ready," someone said.

"You're safe," Powell whispered one last time.

The overhead light did not flicker; the machine gave a brief, confirming tone.

Her eyes widened.

The hum surged, and a single tear slid from the corner of her eye into her hairline, cooling against her skin.

Chapter 17

"And how is she today?" she asked.

Holly hadn't meant for the question to come out sounding accusatory, but it hung there between them anyway. She sat forward in the chair across from Dr. Powell's desk, her hands clasped too tightly in her lap.

The office was quieter than she expected; just the muted ticking of a wall clock and the soft whir of the building's ventilation system.

Dr. Powell folded his hands loosely on the desk. He did not answer immediately, which only made the silence stretch.

"They had to sedate her," he said at last.

Holly's gaze dropped briefly to the edge of the desk, where a thin stack of forms sat partially tucked beneath the file. Her name appeared more than once, looping and familiar, the ink steady in a way she didn't feel now.

Her fingers curled back into her lap.

Her attention shifted across the surface of the desk as if she might find something there that contradicted him. The lamp cast a warm circle of light over a stack of neatly aligned files. A framed photograph stood near the corner, angled slightly toward the chair across from him — a conference room, a podium, a banner in the background she couldn't quite read from where she sat. Powell stood in the image, mid-speech, name badge clipped to his jacket.

She lifted her head.

"Because she attacked someone?"

"Yes," he said, "One of the orderlies. He was doing a routine check."

Holly absorbed it without blinking.

"When did it start getting worse?" Holly asked.

Powell didn't pretend to misunderstand her. "After the anniversary coverage resurfaced."

The articles.

The interview.

The renewed interest.

Holly's mouth went dry.

"I thought exposure would help," she said, "Talking about it. Facing it."

Powell didn't challenge that.

Her eyes drifted again, not to him but to the frame on his desk. The glass caught the overhead light, obscuring the image for a moment, reflecting only the room back at her. Next to it, a small brass nameplate caught the same light.

Benjamin Powell, M.D.

The name settled heavily in her chest.

"She told me she was seeing someone," Holly said carefully. "She talked about him like…" She stopped herself before finishing the sentence.

Like he saved her.

Like he understood her.

Like he chose her.

Powell's expression did not change, but something in his posture shifted to a quiet brace.

"She has a history of attachment transference," he said.

Holly frowned. "Meaning?"

"It means," he clarified, "that she sometimes experiences the therapeutic relationship as something more personal than it is."

"She's not stupid," Holly said, her voice tightening.

"I'm not suggesting she is."

"Then don't reduce this to her imagination."

Powell's hands remained folded on the desk.

"This pattern isn't new," he asked quietly.

The question landed harder than she expected.

"She was eleven," Holly said. "She watched our father disappear. Of course, she clings to things. Of course, she needs —" She broke off, swallowing down the rest.

"Stability," Powell supplied.

"Yes."

That simple agreement took some of the fight out of her.

"She said he checked on her," Holly continued. "After sessions. That he stayed late at her apartment."

"It's common," he continued. "Patients who anticipate extended treatment sometimes reframe their environment in a way that feels less institutional. More permanent. More personal."

Holly blinked.

"She didn't describe it like a patient suite," she said quietly.

"She wouldn't," Powell replied. "It's easier to live inside something when you rename it."

Holly let that settle.

Apartment.

"She said you came over," Holly continued. "That you'd sit with her."

"I conduct room visits when clinically indicated."

His tone remained even.

Delusional didn't fit anymore, as she finally understood something she hadn't before.

Heather wasn't building a fantasy because she was unstable.

She was building it because she was alone. If this place were going to be permanent — if reassessments stretched into years, if step-down became a word that never arrived — then she would need something inside it that she chose.

Someone.

Holly's hands tightened in her lap.

"She sounded happy," she said, almost to herself. "When she talked about you on the phone."

"She doesn't talk about the nurses," Holly continued. "Or other doctors."

Powell didn't answer right away.

"Patients often gravitate toward a primary provider," he said. "Consistency builds trust."

"She trusts you," Holly replied.

"I would hope so."

"That's not what I meant."

He didn't look away from her.

"Trust," he said evenly, "is necessary for treatment to work."

"And if the treatment never ends?"

The question slipped out softer than she intended.

Powell didn't hesitate. "Then stability becomes the goal."

The clock ticked.

Outside the office, a cart rolled past in the hallway. The wheels hummed briefly against the tile and faded.

There it was — the answer she was going to get.

Everything about him was measurable, reasonable, contained. There was nothing improper in his answers, nothing personal she could isolate or challenge without sounding unstable herself.

Holly rose to her feet. She pressed her hands against the smooth fabric of her coat and made her way to the door. Her fingers wrapped around the cold, metallic handle.

She cracked it open just enough for the pale hallway to slip inside.

She paused.

Then she looked back at him.

"She believes you love her," Holly added. "All of you."

This time, she didn't soften it.

Powell's expression didn't change.

"I believe she is ill," he replied.

Holly held his gaze a moment longer.

Then she gave a single nod.

She pulled the door open the rest of the way and stepped into the hallway.

Chapter 18

Reality settled around her in stages as the office door closed behind her. The latch caught with a quiet finality that was louder than it should have been, though the hallway itself remained unchanged. The same pale walls stretched ahead in either direction, broken only by identical doors and framed notices that explained visiting hours and patient guidelines in calm, reassuring language.

A staff member pushed a utility cart briefly across the floor before turning a corner and disappearing.

Holly stood there, hoping the conversation behind that door might reopen and call her back inside. The quiet efficiency of the building continued uninterrupted, each part of it operating with practiced rhythm. Eventually, she turned away and began walking toward the exit.

The first security door released with a muted click as she approached, the lock disengaging automatically before she reached the handle. She pushed it open and passed through, the door closing softly at her back. Ahead, the reception area waited with its low counter and neatly stacked forms. A clipboard lay open beside the desk where visitors signed themselves in and out, the pen attached by a thin plastic cord that stretched slightly when she lifted it. Holly wrote her name on the line beside the time of departure, the ink dragging faintly across the paper before settling into the page. The receptionist glanced up only briefly, offering a polite nod before returning her attention to the computer screen.

"Have a good evening," she said behind the screen.

Holly nodded once. "You too."

Beyond the desk, the final door stood closed. When Holly reached it, the latch released with another quiet click, and the door opened outward to the late afternoon air.

Warm air met her immediately, carrying the dry scent of pavement and the faint sweetness of freshly cut grass. The sky stretched wide and pale above the building, streaked with thin clouds that drifted slowly across the sun. The sudden openness of it was almost disorienting after the contained quiet of the hallways behind her.

The door closed behind her with a soft mechanical seal.

From where she stood, the building looked different from the way it had from the inside. The brick exterior and wide windows gave it the appearance of something modern and welcoming, softened by landscaping and careful design. A narrow row of shrubs lined the walkway. A sign near the entrance listed the facility's departments in clean lettering meant to reassure visitors that everything inside operated under calm and professional care.

Holly stepped off the walkway and started toward the parking lot.

To her right, partially hidden behind a low hedge, the enclosed patio came into view.

She slowed without meaning to.

The patio had been designed to resemble a small courtyard, an open square bordered by a tall black fence that curved slightly at the top. Inside were several iron chairs and a narrow table positioned near the wall. A strip of carefully maintained plants ran along one edge, their leaves bright against the pale concrete beneath them.

The gate that led inside remained closed, a small lock fastening it neatly against the frame.

No one occupied the space now.

Holly remembered Heather sitting there during her first visit, holding a paper cup between both hands while she watched the wind move through the trees beyond the fence. She had tilted her head slightly, breathing in the air with a thoughtful expression.

"It smells different out here," she had said quietly.

At the time, Holly had simply nodded.

Now the patio looked smaller than she remembered.

A staff member crossed the far end of the enclosure carrying a clipboard, pausing briefly to check something against the page before continuing toward the side entrance.

Holly turned away and continued toward her car.

Gravel shifted beneath her shoes as she stepped off the pavement. The parking lot was half full, rows of vehicles sitting in quiet lines beneath the afternoon sun. A delivery van idled near the service entrance at the far end of the building. Beyond the lot, the land opened into fields that rolled gently toward the distant road.

She reached into her bag for her keys as she walked.

Halfway across the lot, something made her look up.

The second floor extended along the building, lined with a series of elongated rectangular windows. Most were simply mirrors of the sky above and the soft, drifting clouds beyond. The sunlight poured in at a slant, transforming several panes into reflective surfaces that caught the light beautifully.

The movement was instinctive.

And then she saw her.

Heather stood behind one of the windows near the center of the row.

She simply stood there, framed by the pale interior of the corridor behind her.

Still.

Watching.

Holly slowed to a stop beside her car.

She wasn't sure if Heather could see her through the reflection. The sunlight made it difficult to tell what was visible from the inside. Holly shifted to the side, angling herself away from the glare.

Heather didn't move.

Her posture was relaxed, as if she had been standing there for some time. Her arms hung loosely at her sides. Her expression was impossible to read from the distance.

Holly's hand lifted before she consciously decided to move.

The small gesture was barely more than an acknowledgment.

Heather didn't respond.

Holly realized something that made the stillness between them feel different.

Heather's gaze was fixed somewhere beyond the parking lot.

As if the world outside the building had flattened into something distant and theoretical, a place she could see but no longer reach.

Holly lowered her hand slowly.

Heather remained where she was, standing behind the glass as if the world outside the building were something distant she could observe but no longer reach. The afternoon light shifted across the window, washing her outline in reflection until Holly could barely distinguish where the sky ended, and Heather began.

A figure appeared several steps back from the window.

The orderly approached at an unhurried pace, his posture calm and practiced. He said something Holly couldn't hear, the words lost behind the glass and the distance between them.

Heather didn't react immediately.

Only when he reached her did she turn her head, acknowledging his presence without surprise.

He rested a hand lightly on her elbow.

Heather's gaze shifted, aligning with Holly's.

Not searching.

Not pleading.

Just noticing.

And then the moment slipped away.

The orderly steered her away from the window. Heather followed his lead, taking small, hesitant steps as he directed her down the corridor.

Her figure receded slowly until the hallway swallowed her from view.

The window filled again with nothing but sky.

Holly lingered beside the car, her hand resting against the door. The sunlight had shifted slightly, brightening the glass until it reflected the clouds drifting slowly overhead. From this distance, there was no sign that anyone had been standing there at all.

The parking lot remained quiet around her.

Holly opened the car door and slid into the driver's seat.

The interior smelled faintly of warm fabric and dust heated by the afternoon sun. Her hands rested loosely against the steering wheel.

Holly started the engine.

The car hummed to life beneath her hands as she shifted into reverse and backed slowly out of the space. Gravel crackled beneath the tires.

At the end of the drive, she paused before pulling onto the road.

She glanced into the rearview mirror, back toward the second floor.

The windows caught the sunlight and flashed white.

Then the angle changed as the car turned, and the building disappeared behind the trees.

I showed you, but you refused to see. Eighteen.

The Weight of Fire: Teaser

The investigator had expected this to be a simple follow-up, the kind that ended with a few answers, a signed report, and a return to the newest murder file waiting on his desk.

"I've tried contacting the orderly who was attacked over at Smithsdale Hospital," the officer said, glancing over from the driver's seat. "No answer. No call back."

The investigator didn't respond immediately. He watched the road ahead, one hand resting loosely against the door. "Then we stop by his place."

The Crown Vic rolled to a stop at the sign before turning onto the main strip of town. Late afternoon light stretched long across the storefront windows, catching on faded signs and empty sidewalks. Smithsdale always carried that quiet, suspended feeling as if something had already happened and the town simply hadn't caught up to it yet.

They passed a gas station with flickering lights, a diner with only half its windows glowing, and a row of closed shops that hadn't changed in years. When they turned into the narrow lot behind the buildings, the apartment complex came into view, slumped and worn as if time had settled heavily into its bones.

Peeling paint clung to the exterior in curling strips. Rusted railings sagged along the walkways, and several windows were patched with cardboard or plastic.

"Are you sure this is it?" the officer asked, already pushing the door open.

The investigator checked the address on his phone and nodded. "Matches what the hospital gave us."

He stepped out and slipped his sunglasses into his coat pocket, his gaze lifting toward the upper floors. The unit was on the third floor.

The stairwell greeted them with a wall of heat and stale air. No ventilation — just the trapped weight of everything that had passed through it and never left. Their footsteps echoed as they climbed, the sound hollow against the narrow walls.

Somewhere behind one of the doors, a child cried; high, sharp, and quickly muffled. The sound lingered just long enough to make the silence that followed feel heavier.

Dark stains streaked upward along the walls.

"Jesus," the officer muttered.

They continued up, the air growing heavier with each step.

By the time they reached the third floor, both men had slowed.

The officer knocked.

"Eli—Smithsdale Police."

He waited, then knocked again, louder this time. "We need to speak with you about the incident at the hospital."

No answer.

He tried the handle.

Locked.

The officer stepped back slightly, about to knock again, when a sound echoed from inside.

He froze, glancing toward the investigator. "Did you hear that?"

The investigator's gaze stayed fixed on the door. "Yeah."

"We're going in."

The first strike splintered the frame. The second cracked it wider, but by the third, the door gave with a sharp snap before opening just enough for them to force their way through.

The apartment itself was small and strangely bare. The kitchen counter was nearly empty, save for a single chipped mug and a stack of unopened mail pushed neatly to one side. No dishes in the sink, or food left out. Nothing suggested someone actually lived there beyond the most basic function.

The living space felt no different. A worn couch pressed flat against the wall. No television. No decorations. No photographs of family, no trace of a life before this place. It was less like a home and more like somewhere a person passed through.

As the officer stepped into the living room, he noticed that the walls didn't match the rest of the room.

Photographs covered them in uneven layers, spreading outward from a central point like something growing. Dozens of them; some pinned carefully, aligned with intention, while others taped quickly, edges curling and corners overlapping.

Heather.

Everywhere.

Photographs at different angles and distances. Some were taken from across a courtyard, others from closer vantage points that made the officer's stomach tighten. There were newspaper clippings mixed in with her name circled in pen — along with a photo of her asleep that lingered just a second too long in his mind.

This was deliberate.

The officer took a slow step forward, his gaze dropping toward the floor.

The carpet was worn down directly in front of the wall. The

fibers had thinned to a darker patch.

"...he just stands here," the officer muttered under his breath.

Something brushed against his leg.

He flinched slightly, glancing down.

An orange cat circled lazily around him, one ear torn along the edge, its body pressing briefly against his pant leg before moving on. The small jingle of its collar broke the stillness just enough to feel out of place.

He crouched slightly, reading the tag.

Terrible.

"...that tracks."

Behind him, the investigator moved through the apartment. His eyes passed over the same details, but lingered on something else.

The kitchen table.

Papers spread across it.

He stepped closer.

Among the papers were printouts. Dates. Times. Locations. Schedules.

And near the edge of the table, half-covered beneath another sheet, sat something older.

A folded document. Creased from being handled too many times.

The investigator pulled it free just enough to see the header.

Case File — Incident Report

The year printed beneath it didn't match anything recent.

His eyes narrowed slightly.

A muffled sound echoed from the hallway. Followed by a dull, uneven bump like something had knocked lightly against wood and settled again.

Both men stilled.

The cat's head snapped toward the hallway, its body going alert. It moved quickly now, crossing the floor and stopping at the closet door, its claws scratching lightly against the surface.

The officer's hand moved instinctively to his holster. "Hold up."

The investigator stepped beside him, eyes fixed on the door.

The scratching continued.

"Someone's in there," the officer said quietly.

The officer reached for the handle, tightened his grip, and pulled the door open.

At first, it didn't register.

A chair.

Something tied.

Then—

A woman.

Her head hung forward, hair falling across her face, her body slack against the restraints. Her wrists were bound tightly behind her back, the rope cutting into the fabric of her sleeves. A strip of cloth had been pulled across her mouth, damp at the edges.

Neither of them moved.

The investigator dropped to his knees in front of her, reaching for her shoulder. His hand brushed against something around her neck.

A lanyard.

He pulled it free just enough to read it.

Donna Bennett - Press

"Donna, can you hear me?" he said quickly, already working at the knot behind her head.

Her eyes fluttered, unfocused at first, then blinked hard against the light.

The cloth came loose.

She inhaled sharply, too fast and too much.

"It's okay," the investigator said. "You're okay."

Her head tipped forward before lifting slightly as she tried to orient herself, gaze drifting past him and into the hallway as if expecting to see someone standing there.

The officer stepped away, already reaching for his radio, his voice low but urgent.

"Dispatch, this is Unit 12. We've got a female victim located at the residence. Conscious, restrained, possible abduction. Suspect is not on scene. Requesting immediate backup and EMS."

Static crackled in response, filling the small apartment for a brief moment before fading again.

The officer turned slowly, scanning the corners of the room.

Behind him, the cat lingered near the closet, tail flicking once before it retreated into the hallway.

"He just kept asking..." Donna's voice was thin, scraped raw.

The investigator leaned closer. "Asking what?"

Her gaze shifted, not quite landing, her breathing still uneven.

"...about her."

Acknowledgments

Writing a novel has always been a dream of mine. As a little girl, I remember sitting at an old clunky Macintosh in my bedroom, spending hours creating short stories. As I grew older, I never imagined I would actually have the courage to put myself out there and publish one.

That said, I could not have done this without the support of my friends and family.

Shauna, thank you for taking the time to proofread early drafts and help refine the story.

Sean, your constant check-ins about my progress kept me accountable and motivated to keep writing.

Nicole, your guidance on the publishing process and your willingness to share your own experience as an author meant more than you know.

And to my husband, Richard, thank you for giving me the time and space to finish this project.

Thank you.

About the Author

K.R. Keen writes psychological suspense that explores memory, perception, and the fragile line between truth and illusion. *The Weight of Glass* is her debut novel.

She first discovered her love for storytelling as a child, spending hours developing stories in her head. Today, that same passion for dark, character-driven narratives continues to shape her work.

Kelsey lives in Kentucky with her family and is usually either reading, writing, or thinking about her next story.

You can connect with me on:

🌐 https://krkeenbooks.wixsite.com/krkeen

www.ingramcontent.com/pod-product-compliance
Lightning Source LLC
Chambersburg PA
CBHW031258130726
47988CB00008B/3413